Roland's voice came out of the darkness

"Don't bother to scream—no one will hear you," he said, and switched on the light.

"If you think you can drive me off with this disgusting behavior," Louise cried, "then you're wrong. Now if you'll kindly stand aside, I'd like to go to my room unmolested."

"Indeed?" His handsome features twisted in a mocking smile. "I wasn't aware that you were in any position to dictate terms."

"This charade is quite ridiculous," she said impatiently. "If this is the only way you can exercise your will over people, then you can't be much of a man!"

Roland strode toward her. She knew she had gone too far with that last remark. He intended to show her how wrong she was.

WELCOME
TO THE WONDERFUL WORLD
OF *Harlequin Romances*

Interesting, informative and entertaining,
each Harlequin Romance portrays an appealing
and original love story. With a varied array
of settings, we may lure you on an African safari,
to a quaint Welsh village, or an exotic Riviera
location—anywhere and everywhere that adventurous
men and women fall in love.

As publishers of Harlequin Romances, we're
extremely proud of our books. Since 1949,
Harlequin Enterprises has built its publishing
reputation on the solid base of quality and
originality. Our stories are the most popular
paperback romances sold in North America; every
month, six new titles are released and sold at
nearly every book-selling store in Canada and the
United States.

A free catalogue listing all Harlequin Romances
can be yours by writing to the

HARLEQUIN READER SERVICE,
(In the U.S.) 1440 South Priest Drive, Tempe, AZ 85281
(In Canada) Stratford, Ontario, Canada N5A 6W2

We sincerely hope you enjoy reading
this Harlequin Romance.

Yours truly,

THE PUBLISHERS
  Harlequin Romances

Château
of Dreams

by

CATHERINE SHAW

Harlequin Books

TORONTO • LONDON • LOS ANGELES • AMSTERDAM
SYDNEY • HAMBURG • PARIS • STOCKHOLM • ATHENS • TOKYO

Original hardcover edition published in 1981
by Mills & Boon Limited

ISBN 0-373-02465-7

Harlequin edition published March 1982

CHAPTER ONE

'LOUISE PETERSON, you need a holiday!'

Edgar Benson placed his two hands affectionately on her shoulders and looked anxiously into her dark brown eyes. They lacked their usual lustre and were faintly dark-ringed. There was a slight droop to her usually merry mouth and a weary slump to her shoulders.

Louise shrugged. 'I can't afford it. I need a commission more than a holiday.'

He bent forward and kissed her forehead lightly. 'Marry me, and you can forget about keeping the wolf from the door.'

An involuntary smile tilted the corners of her mouth. 'I thought you *were* a wolf!'

He chuckled. 'In sheep's clothing, my dearest Louise!'

'No,' Louise refused flatly, as she always did when Edgar proposed.

He lifted his hands from her shoulders, but continued to regard her seriously, unshaken by her rebuff which he was accustomed to. His proposing was almost a running joke between them now.

'You're a fool, Louise,' he said softly. 'A woman can't live without love any more than a man can. Where's the sense in carrying a torch all your life for Paul? A career is no substitute for . . .'

'I'm not carrying a torch . . . oh, do stop lecturing me!' interrupted Louise irritably.

5

Edgar sighed. 'You *are* touchy today! You are definitely tired. You've worked hard for this exhibition, and now you're biting your nails in case it doesn't go well. I'm telling you, Louise, it will go well, and you'll get commissions. So stop worrying!'

She grimaced apologetically. 'Sorry. I wish I had your faith. I know I'm a worrier. I can't help it . . . and, Edgar, I do so want to be a success.'

She glanced around the small West End gallery that Edgar owned, empty now, but at any moment it would begin filling with people attending the preview of an exhibition of contemporary portrait painters. A dozen of Louise's most recent paintings and sketches were among the more illustrious names.

Her speciality was children, but she sometimes painted other portraits too. She walked slowly along the wall where her work was displayed, and surveyed it dispassionately, but underneath her calm exterior, her heart was beating fast. This was her first West End exhibition.

It was all Edgar's idea. She had met him at art school where he had been a lecturer. Later, he had hung a couple of her pictures in the Profile Gallery, and to her astonishment, had sold them. Louise had been jubilant. Both had been portraits.

But Edgar had said, 'Fluke. People don't buy portraits as often as other paintings, not unless they're the Man in the Helmet by Rembrandt or Woman with the Hat by Matisse! What they do buy is portraits of themselves. As you have talent in that direction, my dear Louise, commissions are what you need.'

'How do I get commissions?' she had asked, daunted. She hadn't the slightest idea where to begin, but Edgar had said generously:

'Leave that to me!'

Not long afterwards he had persuaded her to give up her routine job in a commercial art studio and concentrate on producing a dozen good paintings for an exhibition he was planning in the spring. Because she trusted him, Louise obeyed, but now that the exhibition was a reality she had grave misgivings. It was not that she wanted success for its own sake. She just longed to make her living at what she was happiest doing—painting pictures.

Edgar's voice at her elbow jerked her out of her reverie. He smiled at her reassuringly. 'Too late for last-minute touches!' He squeezed her arm. 'I bet you'll have at least one commission by the end of the evening. I've invited all the right sort of people. You must chat 'em up!'

'You're too good to me,' Louise answered, and felt guilty because there was no way she could repay her debt to him. Momentarily, she was tempted to say right there and then that she would marry him, but Edgar was moving away. The guests were beginning to arrive. This evening's preview cocktail party was for invited guests only. Tomorrow the gallery would be open to the public as usual.

Louise sighed. Perhaps she ought to marry Edgar. She had known him long enough—since long before Paul even . . . The picture she was staring at blurred and Paul's face smiled momentarily at her from the frame. It was three years since he had crashed his motorcycle into a tree. But it wasn't, she thought dully, that she still carried a torch for him, as Edgar had said.

In fact, when she examined her feelings honestly, she had none. The shock, the grief, the terrible aching disappointment, had dulled with time, leaving a yawning emptiness to grow unchecked. She wasn't still in love with Paul. She didn't constantly long for him in any sense, physical or otherwise. Sometimes she wondered if she had even been in love with him at all. His death, however, had left a vacuum she could not fill—that Edgar could not fill. She had started going out with other men more than a year ago, but none of her relationships had lasted long. Her feelings for Edgar, she knew only too well, were no more than friendly affection.

'You're frightened,' he had accused once. 'Frightened to take the risk.'

He was probably right, Louise thought. Perhaps she was afraid of loving and losing again. Edgar would be a good husband, and maybe she would learn to love him eventually, but . . . She smiled to herself. Edgar would probably faint if she ever said yes!

People were filling the gallery now and, afflicted with sudden nervousness, Louise vanished to the powder room. No one else was there and she stood for a moment regarding her reflection in the long mirror as though appraising a stranger. In the new fashionable pearl grey silk dress she had bought for the occasion, her slight form seemed even more insubstantial than usual and her dark shoulder-length hair framed a paler than usual face. There *were* rings under her large dark brown eyes, she decided, taking a closer look. Edgar was right, she did look tired. She took out her compact and lightly powdered her nose, then applied fresh pink lipstick. The effect was at least healthier, she thought, grimacing at herself.

Steeling herself, she went back into the gallery, which was filling up fast. Louise had met one or two of the other exhibiting artists, but she knew no one else. Edgar was not immediately visible, so she accepted a glass of champagne from a passing tray and mingled, trying to look more at ease than she felt, while wishing fervently that she was at home, curled up in front of her little electric fire, in an old sweater and jeans with a good book. Among the couture clothes and furs she felt out of place, and wondered how she dared to set herself up as a painter of portraits. She was totally unknown. No one was going to risk giving her a commission. There were heaps of far better artists.

All Edgar's earlier encouragement meant little to Louise as she watched the animated crowd—clustering more around the canapés and the champagne, she thought, than the pictures. 'You've talent, Louise,' echoed Edgar's voice in her head. 'You just need a couple of good commissions, then the word will get around and you'll have more work than you can handle, you'll see.' She had been a fool, she thought, to believe him.

She spotted Edgar at last, on the other side of the gallery, with a party of smart people, but she felt too shy to go over and join them. Instead she found herself drifting back to her own small section of the exhibition. Her pictures of children were mostly based on sketches she had done from life in the parks, or at the zoo, even in trains and buses, or peering through schoolyard railings. She felt wretched. They were awful! She might as well go straight down to the employment agency and go back to being a commercial artist. She might as well forget about being a portrait painter.

Three or four people were looking at her paintings.

Louise longed to hear what they were saying, yet feared it. She moved closer, drawn irresistibly. She did not have to stand too close to hear what a rather beautiful, expensively dressed blonde woman was saying in clear ringing tones to a tall, dark-haired man beside her.

'I've never seen such delightful studies of children, have you, Roland? They're so . . . so alive! What's the artist's name?'

The man thumbed through the catalogue. 'Louise Peterson.' He seemed bored.

'A woman! I might have guessed. She has a special understanding of children . . . perhaps she has some of her own. She certainly captures the effervescence of childhood exquisitely!' She looked eagerly at her companion. 'Don't you think so?'

'Mmm,' he murmured non-committally, and began to move away. At the same moment his glance strayed past his blonde companion, whom Louise assumed was his wife, and his deep-set grey eyes encountered hers.

Louise felt a curious sense of shock, an inexplicable feeling that she knew the man well, and yet she was certain that she had never set eyes on him in her life before. He was not a man you could forget easily. He was a large man, with dark waving hair brushed back from a broad forehead and swooping to a slight widow's peak. Heavy brows and extraordinarily thick lashes shadowed his piercing grey eyes. There was something compelling yet intimidating in his expression.

Louise quickly looked away, and feeling suddenly stifled in the warm atmosphere, she drifted towards the door, leaving the hubbub behind her. All at once she could not bear it any longer. Even the extravagant praise she had just overheard did not lift her spirits. She slipped out into the street, and walked swiftly away from the gallery, not stopping until she reached Piccadilly. There, the swirl of traffic and the kaleidoscope of lights seemed to swallow her up, spinning her like a leaf in a breeze. Only when she shivered and realised she had forgotten her coat did the full impact of what she had done sink in.

Edgar would be furious! What if someone—the blonde woman, for instance—wanted to meet her and she was not there? She had probably spoiled her chances. She stood uncertainly on the kerb, but she simply could not go back. She turned resolutely towards Green Park Underground station and caught the tube home.

In her tiny flat which was more of a bedsitting-room-cum-studio than a flat, with a minute kitchen and bathroom, she made a cup of coffee and slumped into her armchair. She felt shaky and the cup wobbled on the saucer.

'Maybe I should take a holiday,' she murmured to herself. She had worked hard to finish the pictures in time for the exhibition, and she knew she hadn't been eating or sleeping properly lately. Perhaps a few days up in Scotland with Aunt Carrie would restore her vitality. Her brow puckered. She could afford that much. She would look for a job when she came back. She could relax and paint a few landscapes for a change at Aunt Carrie's . . .

Her thoughts were weaving enthusiastically around this new plan of spending a week or two with Aunt Carrie, with lots of good food and healthy walking on the moors with her aunt and the dogs, when the phone rang. Louise started guiltily. It was bound to be Edgar.

Reluctantly she picked up the receiver, feeling rather sheepish now about her behaviour. 'Hello . . .'

His voice came down the line like claps of thunder. 'Louise! You renegade! You traitor! You nincompoop! What on earth made you run out on me?'

Louise quailed, but she said, 'I'm sorry, Edgar . . . I . . . I don't rightly know. Sort of stage fright, I suppose. I was terrified someone might want to talk to me—and afraid no one would . . .'

'You're a prize goose!'

There was a pause, then Louise said, 'Well, I don't imagine it mattered . . .'

An exclamation of exasperation from Edgar cut her off. 'Of course it mattered!'

'But nobody asked . . .'

'Wrong! Several people asked if you were there. But, for heaven's sake, I told you not to expect anything more than that at the preview. It might be weeks before someone thinks it over and decides to commission you. People don't order portraits like potatoes!'

Louise was determined not to indulge in any false optimism. 'Well, I've decided to take that holiday you said I needed,' she told him. 'I'm going up to Scotland to stay with Aunt Carrie.'

'Great idea! That'll put the roses back in those beautiful cheeks and the sparkle in your eyes. When are you leaving?'

'I don't know. I've yet to ring her. If it's convenient, I might as well go right away. Tomorrow or the next day, I expect.'

'Good girl. Now, are you still in your glad rags?'

'Ye-es . . .' she answered.

'Good. I thought you might have been back in jeans and that filthy old sweater you usually paint in! We're going out to dinner—just you and me,' he added, anticipating her objection to a crowd.

But even without a crowd, Louise did not feel like sitting in a restaurant. She wanted to go to bed and sleep. She had suddenly realised how tired she was.

'Edgar, really I'd rather not. It's getting late and . . .'

He sighed. 'All right, I won't press you. What you need is a good night's sleep, my girl. Ring me tomorrow and let me know when you're going, and what your phone number is up there in case I need to get in touch.'

Louise promised she would. When she had put the phone down she went into her tiny kitchen and made herself a cheese sandwich, and squeezed another cup of coffee out of the percolator. It was no good ringing Aunt Carrie tonight, it was her night for playing bridge and she would be out. Louise settled down to watch television for a while, but her eyes kept closing, so she soon went off to bed. When she undressed she was thinking with pleased anticipation of her holiday with her aunt, who had brought her up, but whom she saw all too seldom these days, but when she fell asleep it was on the image of a tall dark-haired man with penetrating grey eyes.

She woke to the sound of the telephone ringing. It was on the table beside her divan bed, so she reached sleepily for the receiver, at the same time noticing with horror that it was after ten o'clock. She had overslept dreadfully.

'Hello . . .' she mumbled, still only half awake.

It was Edgar. 'Louise, great news!' His voice exploded into her ear. 'I think I've got you a commission. Can you go and see Lady Winterhaven tomorrow at ten a.m.?'

'Edgar, just a minute . . .' Louise was flustered by the unexpectedness of it.

'Louise,' he went on, 'she's got four young children and she's absolutely sold on you. She wants you to paint them all—right away!'

Louise felt weak. 'But I'm going for a holiday,' she protested, knowing it sounded foolish. 'You said I needed a holiday, and I do. I couldn't possibly do my best work right now.'

'I know! I told Amber that, but she swept all protests aside. She wants you *now*. She said you can combine having a holiday with working.'

'Edgar, is she a friend of yours?' Louise asked suspiciously.

'Yes. Well, not a close friend. I used to advise her husband on buying paintings.'

'If this is just because you're a friend . . .' Louise objected.

'Louise, stop being so pigheaded and proud! What if it is? But I assure you it isn't. It was her idea entirely and she had no idea you were a protégée of mine. She's suggested that you might like to get to know the children in their home environment before you start painting, and she doesn't care how long you take. What's more, you can name your price. At least that's the impression I got. You can't turn it down, Louise. This is the chance you need. She's very well connected . . .'

'You mean she wants me to live with them?' asked Louise apprehensively. She sat up and hugged the bedclothes around her, fully awake now, but still unable to take it in properly.

'*En famille*, my dear.'

'Where does she live?' Louise felt a lift of interest in spite of herself.

'France.'

'France!' This was a shock.

'Yes. In the Loire Valley. I stayed at the château once. Very picturesque, very peaceful, and perfect painting country. Louise, this is a wonderful opportunity.' He added reproachfully, 'And you don't sound the slightest bit thrilled.'

Louise ran her fingers through her tumbled dark hair and drew her knees up to her chin. 'Edgar, I am ... I really am ... but it's just a bit sudden, and I'm not even properly awake yet. I'm having a bit of difficulty taking it in. I'd already made up my mind to Aunt Carrie and Scottish moors.'

'Well, rapidly unmake it, my dear. This could be the start of your real career. You simply can't turn it down. Four individual portraits she wants, and a group. She also mentioned in passing that she may commission you to paint her late husband as well.'

'*Late* husband?' Louise enquired, slightly startled.

'From photographs, of course,' explained Edgar with a faint chuckle. 'I can see you haven't heard of Sir Peter Winterhaven.'

'Should I have?'

'Not necessarily. You're too young. He was a leading organiser in the French Resistance during World War II, and also a famous sportsman. He won a Gold Medal for fencing at the Berlin Olympics.'

'Bit before my time,' agreed Louise. 'And I'm not very sports-minded.

'Never mind. Neither is Lady Winterhaven. She's

his . . . was his second wife. Very much younger, of course. But you can amuse yourself with Winterhaven family history later. The important thing is, can you be at Number 3, Bellgrove Mansions, Knightsbridge, at ten tomorrow morning? She's staying in town with her mother at the moment. Now you must have heard of the Farrington-Granges?'

'Shoes,' said Louise promptly.

'Good girl! Sir Lennox Farrington-Grange, now deceased, was in shoes, textiles, plastics, just about everything. Lady Farrington-Grange is a byword on charity committees.'

'It all sounds out of my depth,' said Louise doubt-fully.

'Nonsense. Just be your nice sweet natural self and all will go swimmingly. You'll have a fabulous holiday and come home with a fat cheque and probably introductions to any number of future clients. Amber—Lady Winterhaven—is a charming person, no side at all, and if she likes you and your work, you won't be ignored, you can be sure.'

'It all sounds a bit like a fairy tale.' Louise was beginning to feel excited as the realisation began to sink in, but apprehensive too.

'It may well be,' agreed Edgar. He added anxiously, 'You'll go?'

'Yes . . .' Why she hesitated, Louise could not be quite sure. Wasn't it after all what she wanted? This was the chance she had been hoping for, the breakthrough that could establish her reputation, and yet now that it was within reach, she was aware of a familiar sinking feeling.

'Louise . . .' coaxed Edgar softly. 'Stop being afraid

and take the plunge. The water will be very warm, I assure you!'

Louise laughed. Edgar read her so accurately. She *was* afraid. Here was the opportunity she had longed for, and now she was nervous. She couldn't help it. She was just made that way, and she always had to fight it. 'All right,' she said decisively, 'I'll call at Bellgrove Mansions in the morning.'

'Good girl!' approved Edgar. 'You've really got plenty of get-up-and-go, Louise. All you need is a little more self-confidence.' He added firmly, 'And when you're through, come straight on here, and I'll take you out for a celebration lunch.'

CHAPTER TWO

THE next morning Louise was up early, determined to be punctual for her appointment in Knightsbridge. The big problem was what to wear. She looked through her limited wardrobe several times, uncertain which outfit would be the most suitable. Eventually she chose her new tweed suit, as the weather was chilly despite spring making its first tentative appearance in the parks and gardens.

The tweed was a heather mixture and with it Louise teamed a deep pink shirt which reflected some colour into her still pale cheeks. The dark shadows beneath her eyes were not so obvious this morning, she noticed with satisfaction as she brushed her hair to a satiny gloss, and when presently applying a little mascara to her lashes and shaping her eyebrows deftly.

When she went downstairs, she met Mrs Perkins who lived on the ground floor and worked in the fashion department of a big store. Smiling approvingly, she looked Louise up and down. It was she who had helped her buy the suit.

'Charming! That colour definitely suits you. And the blouse teams perfectly. You've a good eye for colour, Louise . . . but of course, you should have, shouldn't you, being an artist.' She came closer. 'You look better today, more your old self. The exhibition was a success, I hope?'

Louise held up a hand with her first and middle fingers crossed. 'I'm hoping so,' she said with a smile.

'I'm just off to an interview with a Lady Winterhaven who wants someone to paint portraits of her children.'

Mrs Perkins eyebrows shot up. 'Gracious! Already? Well, good luck, my dear.' She added with a sly smile, 'If Lord Winterhaven was doing the interviewing, you'd get the job like a shot. He'd be bound to be captivated!'

Louise blushed. 'He was Sir . . . and I'm afraid he's dead.'

'Oh, dear! Well, anyway, all the best, dear.'

'Thank you, Mrs Perkins,' said Louise, and hurried on her way.

She felt reassured that at least she looked presentable. There was quite a spring in her step as she swung jauntily down the street towards the tube station. A blackbird was singing lustily in a plane tree in the little square she had to cross, and the sound lifted her spirits even higher. She kept her fingers crossed, but there was a feeling deep inside her that today marked a new beginning.

Some of her confidence fled, however, when she finally confronted the impressive façade of Bellgrove Mansions. In the entrance there was a list of apartments with a bellpush beside each. Louise rang the one beside number three. Almost immediately a woman's voice through the security intercom enquired who she was, and when told, invited her to come up. As instructed, Louise pushed the door, which swung open on automatic release, and found herself in a deeply carpeted foyer opposite a lift. She took a deep breath and went up to the third floor.

A smiling maid greeted her at the apartment door. Louise glanced around surreptitiously as she was led

through the entrance hall into a drawing room furnished mainly with antiques.

'Lady Winterhaven won't be long,' said the maid.
'She's with the baby, Melissa, at the moment. The
doctor's there. Melissa had a tummy upset last
night.'

'I'm so sorry . . .' murmured Louise, quaking a
little as she glanced around the room. She was out of
her depth all right amid all this. But she remembered
Edgar's firm injunctions earlier that morning when
he had rung to encourage her. 'Don't chicken out, or
I might not speak to you again!'

She would not chicken out, she thought resolutely,
even though at that minute she had a strong desire
to cut and run just as she had at the preview of the
exhibition. She owed it to Edgar not to do anything
so foolish. He had shown enormous, and probably
undeserved faith in her, even risking money on her,
so she owed it to him not to treat such a golden
opportunity as this lightly.

The maid left her sitting edgily on a satin brocade
chair, clutching her handbag as though it contained
all her worldly possessions. From time to time she
nervously fingered her hair back behind her ears,
and tried to stop herself anxiously running her tongue
over her lips. She wished Lady Winterhaven would
hurry.

She concentrated on looking at the pictures, most
of which were traditional landscapes, chiefly
Victorian, and after a few minutes was reminded of
the purpose of her visit by the sound of the door
opening. She glanced across and saw it being pushed
open very slowly. She was about to stand up, assum-
ing it was Lady Winterhaven—but Lady
Winterhaven would surely not giggle like that, nor

would she say in a loud stage whisper, and a boy's tone, 'I say, she's not a bad-looking bird, is she?'

'Shhh!' whispered someone else. More stifled giggles followed.

Louise smiled to herself, as she caught a glimpse of blonde curls. 'Why don't you come in?' she called in a friendly voice.

There was a moment of dead silence. Louise thought she must have frightened them away, but the next moment the door opened wide and three children marched into the room. The leader was a gangly girl of about ten years old. She was not the giggly one, Louise felt sure. She had brown hair and eyes and a very serious expression. Behind her swaggered a boy of about eight. He had the same brown hair and eyes, and an impish grin. Tagging along behind him was the owner of the blonde curls, a very angelic-looking little girl. A real cherub, thought Louise. She was about four years old.

The eldest faced Louise. 'I must apologise for my brother and sister,' she announced. 'They're very rude children.'

Louise was too startled to know what to reply.

The girl went on, 'Are you Miss Peterson who's going to paint us?'

Louise nodded. 'Yes . . . at least I hope so.'

The girl held out her hand. Louise gravely shook it, and then the boy's and the younger girl's.

'How do you do?' she murmured to each of them.

'How do you do?' said the eldest for all of them.

The boy pushed forward. 'What colours are you going to paint us?'

Louise was again taken aback. 'Oh . . . all different colours, I expect.'

The smallest girl looked pleased. 'Can I be blue

and yellow, please? Blue and yellow are my favourite colours.'

'Well, that will depend on what you're wearing,' said Louise. 'You'll have to ask your mummy if you can wear a blue or a yellow dress.' She added, 'Would you like to tell me your names?'

'I'm Selena,' said the oldest, 'and this is my brother, Simon, and my sister Angela. We've got a baby sister, Melissa, but she's sick and Mummy and the doctor are fixing her up.'

Simon was treating Louise to a very thorough scrutiny as though, she thought uneasily, summing her up and deciding just how far she could be tried. She marked him down as mischievous. There was something about the two girls that seemed vaguely familiar, but she could not place it.

'Will you be coming to the château?' asked Simon.

'Of course she will,' said Selena.

Angela sidled up to Louise's knee. 'Will you play games with us?'

Louise was disarmed by their very direct approach. 'Yes-es, I expect so,' she answered, smiling, captivated by the earnest face turned up to hers. Already she was itching to transfer those angelic features to canvas.

'What sort of games?', demanded Simon, interested.

Louise countered, 'What sort of games do you like?'

'Cops and robbers ... Star Wars ...' said Simon.

'That's rubbish,' said Selena rather grandly, adding, 'We don't watch television all the time.'

'Worse luck,' grumbled Simon under his breath.

Louise looked from one to the other, fascinated by the striking features of Selena, Simon's mischievous expression, and the soft, slightly vague innocence of Angela who, she thought, was aptly named. They would be sheer delight to paint. They were clearly not spoiled little brats, but characterful little individuals. Realising this, Louise felt her reserve begin to melt, and she no longer felt nervous. The challenge of work had banished all thoughts of anything except that she could hardly wait to get started.

'Play a game now,' demanded Angela.

'Oh, I don't think . . .' began Louise. 'Your mother will be here in a minute.'

'Mummy will be ages,' said Simon. 'She fusses like anything over Melissa. She only had diarrhoea. Babies have it all the time.' He screwed up his face in disgust.

Louise's eyebrows rose, but she said nothing. Selena rebuked, 'Melissa's delicate like I was.'

'We might as well play something,' urged Angela appealingly.

'All right, what would you like to play?' asked Louise, feeling it was diplomatic to keep on the right side of the children since she was going to need their co-operation later, but hoping they would not suggest anything too boisterous.

'One of your games,' suggested Angela shyly.

Louise was stuck. She could not think of anything suitable. What games had she played in her childhood that would fit this rather unusual occasion? All she could think of in the static category was I Spy. She was afraid it might be too tame for these rather sophisticated children, but they jumped at the idea.

'Bags first!' said Simon.

'She should go first,' put in Selena. 'She thought of it and besides, she's a guest.'

To avoid any argument, Louise went first. They became so absorbed in the game that they did not hear the door open. Simon was giving a loud whoop of delight because he had guessed a particularly difficult object when Louise suddenly became aware of a presence in the room and jumped up. A tall fair woman came smilingly across to her, her hand extended in welcome. Louise's mouth dropped open in surprise. It was the blonde woman she had seen in the gallery yesterday, the one who had enthused over her paintings. So, she thought irrelevantly, the dark-haired man couldn't have been her husband. Edgar had said he was dead.

'Miss Peterson, how do you do?' Lady Winterhaven clasped Louise's hand warmly in beringed fingers. 'I do apologise for keeping you waiting so long. I hope these imps have not been annoying you. I told Maida to keep them out of your way.' She laughed engagingly. 'I didn't want you to be put off!'

'How do you do, Lady Winterhaven,' Louise murmured, her nervousness returning. It was obvious the woman had not noticed her yesterday, as she did not appear to recognise her. She was as beautiful, Louise thought, as she had decided then. She had a delicate porcelain beauty, blonde and fragile with deep violet blue eyes and a slender figure. She must be at least thirty, Louise judged, and yet she didn't look a day over twenty-five. Louise added quickly, 'I've enjoyed getting to know Selena, Simon and Angela.'

'We've been playing I Spy!' piped up Angela.

Lady Winterhaven rolled her eyes. 'Poor Miss

Peterson!' She turned to her brood. 'Now, children, out! Miss Peterson and I have to talk.'

The maid came bustling into the room and shepherded the children out. At the door Angela turned and gave Louise a small smiling wave which she found quite touching.

'Children!' exclaimed Lady Winterhaven. 'If I'd known I would be left to bring them up on my own, I might have had a few second thoughts. But Peter was all for a big happy family . . .' Suddenly her eyes filled with tears, and Louise felt embarrassed. She hardly knew what to say.

She heard herself murmuring, 'I'm so sorry about your husband, Lady Winterhaven. I . . . I understand how you feel. I lost my fiancé three years ago . . .'

She wished she had not blurted out the last bit. Lady Winterhaven was not interested in her loss, and she had blundered by mentioning it. But, to her surprise, Lady Winterhaven said thoughtfully, 'It's strange, but I had the oddest feeling, looking at your paintings, that you and I would understand each other.' She smiled jerkily. 'Don't think me silly and sentimental. I've quite faced up to Peter's death. It's just . . . the emptiness that overcomes me now and again.'

'I know,' said Louise simply. 'I feel like that too sometimes.'

They smiled sympathetically at each other and Louise had the feeling that she had just made a friend.

'Well, enough of this maudlin talk,' said Lady Winterhaven briskly. 'Let's get down to business. Maida will bring us some tea shortly, but meanwhile

we might as well settle a few details. Edgar ... Mr
Benson has told me all about you, and since Peter
spoke highly of his judgment where art is concerned,
I trust his recommendation completely. In any case,
having seen some of your work myself, I should trust
my own judgment! Now, I take it that since you're
here, you wish to accept the commission?' She
laughed. 'Unless being badgered by my brood has
changed your mind!'

'Not at all. They're delightful children,' said
Louise sincerely. 'I can't wait to start painting
them.'

'There's Melissa too, of course. Poor little baby
isn't well today, but the doctor says it's nothing serious, just a touch of enteritis.'

'I'm sorry . . .'

'Oh, I fuss too much, everyone says. But Melissa is
precious. All babies are! Alas, poor Peter never saw
her—such a perfect little thing she is, too!'

Louise was afraid she was going to get sorrowful
again, so she ventured, 'Edgar mentioned something
about a portrait of your husband.'

'Yes, I did mention it to him.' She regarded Louise
steadily. 'If you don't think it's too much to ask, of
course. You see, he's going to be honoured in our
village. He wouldn't hear of such a thing during his
lifetime. He told them they must wait until he was
dead. Peter was very modest. He said he couldn't
bear to come face to face with himself every time he
walked through the village square!' She laughed, and
there was no sadness, only pride in her eyes now.
'They're not going to erect a statue, thank goodness.
I vetoed that as I think statues are so cold. We've
decided on a nice big portrait to hang in the Town
Hall alongside the Roll of Honour.'

Louise suddenly felt capable of anything. 'I'd love to do it,' she said eagerly.

The maid came in with tea and as they drank it, and ate the tiny crustless sandwiches and warm buttered scones, Lady Winterhaven said, 'I shall be returning to France the day after tomorrow. I should like you to come back with us if you can.'

Louise was taken aback. This was rather precipitate. She wondered if there was any reason for the rush, or if Lady Winterhaven was simply an impulsive person. Something in her expression made Louise uneasy, but she dismissed the feeling as ridiculous.

She said, 'Well, to be honest, that is a bit soon. I really need a few days to fix up things here—my mail, the flat . . . all those little things . . .'

'Yes, yes, yes,' agreed Lady Winterhaven, but she looked rather anxious. 'How soon could you come? I'll arrange your airline ticket and . . .'

Louise, on a sudden thought, interrupted her. 'No . . . please . . . I'd rather drive down, if you don't mind. It won't take much longer, and I'll have rather a lot of gear to bring with me.'

'Of course, what a good idea. Then you'll be able to see something of the countryside too, while you're with us. I mustn't forget you're on holiday. There's no rush whatsoever and you must relax completely. Peter's picture doesn't have to be ready until September. His biography will be coming out then and that's when we'll be having the dedication in Les Deux Croix.'

Louise wondered why, then, all the rush now. She said, 'I'm sure I shall have completed the task long before then!'

Lady Winterhaven rose and went over to a bureau.

'I'm sure Mother has . . . yes, here it is.' She came back and unfolded a map. 'Now, let me show you how to get to the Château des Ormeaux.'

They pored over the map for a few moments and then Lady Winterhaven said, 'I think that's all. Unless there's anything you want to ask?'

'I don't think so,' said Louise. Her fee had not yet been discussed, but she did not like to mention it.

Lady Winterhaven smiled. 'Your name is Louise, isn't it? I may call you that, I hope. And I should like you to call me Amber. I'm not fond of formality, especially among friends.'

Her smile was so genuine that Louise was deeply touched. To be regarded as a friend when they scarcely knew each other was a real compliment. 'Thank you very much,' she said.

At that moment the door opened and a brown haired, athletic-looking girl of about twenty-five popped her head around the door.

'Excuse me, Lady Winterhaven, but could you spare a minute . . . Melissa is fretting again and you seem to be the only one who can quieten her today.'

Amber Winterhaven leapt up, her lovely face creased with worry. 'Yes, Philippa, I'll come straight away.' She turned to Louise hastily. 'I'm so sorry, I shall have to leave you for a few minutes. Do help yourself to another cup of tea. I hope I won't be long.' She stopped and looked stricken anew. 'Goodness, we haven't discussed your fee. We'll do that just as soon as I get back.'

She disappeared with the girl, who Louise supposed was the children's nanny. Louise poured herself another cup of tea and sat back in her chair and contemplated her unfamiliar surroundings. Minutes passed. She studied the map again, and was just re-folding it to push into her handbag when a door opened, not the one Amber had departed through, but the one she herself had entered by.

Louise glanced up, and was astonished to see the tall dark man who had been with Amber Winterhaven at the Profile Gallery two evenings ago. He seemed equally startled to see her. Their eyes met and held for a long moment and, subjected to his frank appraisal, Louise felt a confusion that was alien to her, a quickening of her pulse and an odd tingling in her spine. All her nervousness returned.

He came nonchalantly into the room. 'I beg your pardon,' he said, not taking his eyes off her. 'I didn't realise there was anyone here.'

'Lady Winterhaven was called away. The baby was crying.' Louise's voice shook quite unnecessarily. 'She won't be long.'

He stood near her, treating her to a lengthy admiring look. 'And whom have I the pleasure of meeting?' he enquired, adding, 'I'm Roland Winterhaven.'

Louise extended her hand and felt it clasped in warm, strong fingers that sent a new shiver down her backbone. 'I'm Louise Peterson,' she said.

Instantly a guarded look replaced his approval of her. 'Louise Peterson!' The exclamation was uttered low as her fingers slid from his palm. 'The artist?'

Louise nodded. 'Yes.' And then, because his gaze disconcerted her, she rushed on, 'As a matter of fact, there's no need for me to disturb Lady Winterhaven further. I might as well go. Perhaps you'd tell her . . .' She stood up, but he did not move, nor did he speak, but merely by his largeness seemed to bar her way.

She and Lady Winterhaven could talk about
money later, Louise thought, for some reason not
relishing doing so in front of this man. The thought
embarrassed her in any case, even where only Lady
Winterhaven was concerned. She said, 'Lady
Winterhaven has my telephone number, in case . . .'

Her slight move forward was deflected by his raised
hand, the palm towards her. 'Just a moment, Miss
Peterson,' he said, in an authoritative tone. 'Perhaps
you would kindly explain what all this is about?'

His tone nettled Louise. What business was it of
his? However, she could think of no reason why he
should not know, so she explained briefly why she
was there, aware all the time of his increasing annoyance, the deepening of the furrows in his brow.

Finally, in a voice as steely as his gaze, he said,
'I'm very much afraid, Miss Peterson, that there's
been an unfortunate misunderstanding. It's just as
well I returned when I did.'

'Misunderstanding?' Her voice was barely a
squeak. Her slight feeling of unease earlier turned
now to one of impending disaster.

'I'm afraid it's impracticable for you to come to
the Château des Ormeaux at the moment. Quite
impossible, in fact.'

'Impossible!' Louise was beginning to feel like an
echo, but she was so stunned she did not know what
to say.

He placed his hand apologetically on her arm.
'I'm so sorry. Lady Winterhaven has evidently forgotten that there'll be workmen at the château for
the next few weeks, while she's in England. It would
be most inconvenient . . .'

'But she said she was going home in two days,'
Louise argued.

'As I said, she has clearly forgotten. She usually stays in England for several weeks in any case. No doubt the excitement of meeting you put it out of her mind.' With his hand on her arm he began quite purposefully to guide her towards the door.

'Where do you live?' he asked abruptly.

Louise told him.

'Then I shall drive you home. That's the least I can do to recompense you for wasting your time.'

Louise swallowed hard. She was shattered, and her disappointment filled her like a weighty stone. She found it hard to believe that Lady Winterhaven could have forgotten. 'I . . . I think I ought to see Lady Winterhaven,' she faltered, hoping Amber would come back, that some new arrangement could be made.

But she didn't, and Roland Winterhaven said, 'If she's with the baby she's probably forgotten all about you too! I'll explain to her. There's no need for you to be held up. Perhaps later on she'll get in touch with you again and make other arrangements.' He smiled reassuringly. 'She's very anxious to have you paint the children's portraits.'

The door was opened and he was very determinedly guiding her through it, the essence of politeness, but, she could not help thinking, with a ruthless set to his mouth. She could scarcely dig her heels in and insist on seeing Lady Winterhaven again, so there seemed no alternative but to acquiesce with this man's arrogant manipulation.

Roland Winterhaven said, 'My car is parked in front of the building.' They were through the front door of the apartment now. Louise cast a last hopeful look over her shoulder, but there was no one around, not even one of the children. The faint sound of a baby crying reached her ears, indicating that Lady Winterhaven was still very firmly occupied.

She turned to her companion, resentful of the hand that held her arm, lightly though he did so. He was deliberately escorting her out of the apartment, and as hurriedly as possible, even though she had been the first to suggest she might as well go. Suddenly Louise remembered her lunch date with Edgar.

'I've just remembered, I'm not going straight home,' she said. 'I have an appointment, and I can go straight there on the tube, so there's no need for you to come down.'

'I shall drive you wherever it is you have to go,' he insisted, and pressed the button for the lift. He was quite determined to see her off the premises, it seemed.

'There's really no need,' she insisted frostily. 'The traffic in the West End will be impossible at this time of day.'

The lift came and he stood aside, holding the doors open for her, then joined her inside.

'It's the least I can do in the circumstances,' he said.

Louise was silent. When they reached the steps leading up to the entrance, she repeated that there was no need for him to drive her. This time he looked steadily at her for a moment, then shrugged.

'Very well, since you insist.' He held out his hand. 'Please again accept my sincere apologies, Miss Peterson. It was delightful meeting you and I hope we'll meet again. I hope you haven't been put to any undue inconvenience because of Lady Winterhaven's slight lapse of memory.' His hand clasped hers very firmly and held it just a shade too long.

A taxi halted and an elderly lady in a fur coat alighted and called out, 'Roland! How lucky! Have you got any change, dear . . . for the taxi?'

'Yes, of course, Lady Farrington-Grange,' he called back, and began fumbling in his pockets. He glanced at Louise. 'Goodbye, Miss Peterson. I shall look forward to meeting you again.' His farewell smile was wide, sincere, almost regretful, and yet, thought Louise, his whole demeanour seemed to indicate heartfelt relief.

She muttered, 'Goodbye,' and fled down the street without a backward look. She felt that in some way she had been made a fool of, and she felt angry at the man who had done it. She made her way to the Profile Gallery, but with a heavy heart. It would be a commiseration lunch, she reflected miserably, not the happy celebration she and Edgar had expected.

CHAPTER THREE

'NEVER mind,' soothed Edgar, placing his hand over Louise's as they waited for their lunch to arrive. 'Something else will turn up, you'll see. And it isn't final anyway. Amber will get back to you. It's just a temporary postponement, perfectly reasonable.'

Louise shook her head. 'I don't think so. I've got a feeling about it.' She screwed up her face in puzzlement yet again. 'It was all so odd, Edgar. He couldn't get rid of me quickly enough. It was almost as though he had something against me personally.'

Edgar laughed. 'What could he possibly have against you?'

Louise shrugged. 'Nothing.' She looked at him ruefully. 'I'm just not destined to be a portrait painter, Edgar, and I might as well face up to it.'

He squeezed her fingers hard. 'Now, stop that! You mustn't be defeatist, Louise! You'll get another break, I'm sure . . . and soon.'

She smiled at him gratefully. 'I don't deserve your encouragement.'

'No, you don't,' he agreed, but with a cheerful grin. He reached across the table and tilted her chin. 'Look at me! Now what you do is exactly what you planned to do before Lady Winterhaven came along. Off you go to the wilds of Scotland and have a nice restful holiday. By the time you come back I'll probably have a list of people clamouring for you.'

Louise laughed. 'Edgar, you're so nice! And such a consummate liar!'

Louise was not a girl to delude herself. Rather, she tended to sway too far in the other direction. She knew that there were plenty of portrait painters already established, competing for the limited work available. Her chances were very slim. Her only chance, she thought bleakly, had been Lady Winterhaven, and now that was lost.

Roland Winterhaven, heavy-handed and arrogant, had spoiled everything. But it was hardly his fault, she amended. If the château was going to be bristling with workmen, then obviously it was sensible for the family to stay away. It wasn't fair to blame him. It was just that his high and mighty manner had annoyed her. He had seemed so anxious to get rid of her, and to prevent her seeing Amber again. It was rather odd, to say the least.

She held no hopes that she would be contacted again at a later date. Louise had a feeling that having her children's portraits painted would prove to have been just a passing whim of Amber Winterhaven's, or if not, she would forget Louise and choose another artist who took her fancy.

She sighed and shrugged resignedly. What did it matter? There was nothing to be done about it. She would have her holiday with Aunt Carrie as she had previously planned and try to forget the golden opportunity that had evaporated.

'Anyway, I've sold one of your pictures in the exhibition,' announced Edgar, as the waiter arrived with their first course. 'Almost forget to tell you. So we have something to celebrate after all.'

Louise was instantly eager. 'Really? Which one? Who to?'

Edgar eyed her quizzically. 'You know, Louise,

you're a chameleon in your moods. When you're excited, like now, your whole face lights up, and you're really quite beautiful.'

The compliment made Louise blush, especially as the waiter was not out of earshot. He turned to smile at her and give her an admiring glance. She said hastily, 'Edgar, stop flattering me and tell me which picture, and how much?'

'Enough to finance your little excursion to Scotland,' he told her tantalisingly. 'Even after my commission. As a matter of fact it was the Victorian child on a swing. Some old dowager in a fur that reeked of mothballs. She said it reminded her of herself when she was a little girl!' He laughed. 'Perhaps you should concentrate on kitsch for calendars and suchlike!'

'Was it that bad?' Louise did not mind bluntness from Edgar. Where art criticism was concerned he pulled no punches, never flattered, and was always brutally frank. But he knew what he was talking about and she had learned to respect him for it, and to quell the little flares of egotistical indignation that involuntarily rose when he was less than kind about her work.

His hazel eyes were teasing her. 'My dear Louise, would I have hung it in Profile, in one of my most prestigious exhibitions of the year, if it was bad? Surely you have more respect for my judgment, and frankly, even for you, my lovely, I wouldn't compromise my reputation!'

'It's an idea about the calendars, though,' said Louise thoughtfully. 'Maybe I could freelance instead of getting a job in a studio. There are greeting cards, too . . .'

'And chocolate boxes and soap advertisements.' Edgar was still teasing. Then he switched to a serious tone. 'Forget all about such things for a while, Louise, and enjoy your holiday. We'll see what happens afterwards.' He grinned at her mockingly. 'As I said before, if you hate it too much you can always marry me and help run Profile.' A sudden thought struck him. 'Well, I'm damned, why didn't I think of it before? How would you like to do just that?'

'The answer is still no,' said Louise absently. 'You know I can't marry you. I'm not in love with you.'

He brushed that aside. 'I didn't mean that. I meant how about helping me at Profile? I could do with an assistant with your experience and critical eye.'

'You're flattering me again,' said Louise, adding, 'No, Edgar, you've already done too much for me. I don't want any more favours.'

'It would be a favour to me,' he insisted.

She shook her head. 'No, it wouldn't. You've already got Cathy and I wouldn't want to put her nose out of joint. No, Edgar. Thank you, but I couldn't . . .'

He sighed. 'You're a stubborn, proud, incorrigible girl!'

'I'm sorry!'

After the lunch which, although excellent, Louise had had little appetite for, she walked back to the Profile Gallery with Edgar, as he insisted on giving her a cheque for the picture he had sold, right away, despite her protestations that she was not that hard up.

As soon as they walked in, Cathy appeared.

'Oh, good, you're back,' she said. 'I told her you wouldn't be long.'

'Who?' asked Edgar absently, thumbing through some letters on his desk.

'Lady Winterhaven.' Cathy turned to Louise. 'Actually it's you she wants to speak to, Miss Peterson. She rang twice and I said I'd make sure you got the message. She seemed rather het up about something and said it was urgent she talk to you.'

Edgar's eyebrows rose as he looked at Louise. 'She wants to apologise, I expect. Better give her a ring. You might as well keep sweet with her.' He added, 'Do it now from here.'

Although she was reluctant to telephone Lady Winterhaven Louise felt that Edgar was right and she should do so right away. Edgar and Cathy left her alone, and she dialled the number Cathy had written on the message pad. The maid answered.

'It's Louise Peterson,' said Louise. 'I believe Lady Winterhaven wishes to speak to me.'

'Oh, yes, Miss Peterson, just a moment . . .'

Louise waited, feeling a little nervous. It was kind of Lady Winterhaven to want to apologise, a courtesy she had not expected, but she did not know what she was going to say herself. Apologies always embarrassed her.

'Hello, Louise?' Amber Winterhaven's voice breathed relief. 'I've been so anxious to get hold of you. I'm so dreadfully sorry about that misunderstanding this morning.'

'Really, it's quite all right,' said Louise, 'I . . .'

'It isn't all right at all,' broke in Lady Winterhaven emphatically. 'Roland had no right to countermand my plans. He's altogether too high-handed sometimes!'

'But I thought . . .'

'I know. He fobbed you off with some cock-and-bull story about renovators. That was the first I'd heard of it, I swear! In fact we had a blazing row about it. He takes too much . . .' She stopped. 'Louise, it will take too long to explain properly on the telephone, but I promise I will when you come to France. Roland handles my affairs and he takes the job rather too seriously. He's always trying to ride roughshod over me. He knows I won't stand for it.'

Louise was astonished. 'But I thought . . .' she repeated stupidly.

'Forget all that. I've ironed out the misunderstanding. It's the renovating that will be postponed. You must come to France as we planned.' She paused. 'That is if you're not too angry with us.'

Louise felt she was being bounced up and down like a yo-yo. She said limply, 'No, of course not.' Then she added, 'How is the baby?'

'Much better. Poor little mite! I do so hate it when babies are sick. They can't tell you where it hurts!'

Louise smiled. Amber was a delightfully natural person, the sort of person no one could ever say no to, she thought. Yet she had a stubborn side, obviously. She had managed to override Roland Winterhaven, and he had seemed to Louise a supremely difficult man to override. She wondered exactly what his relationship was to Lady Winterhaven.

'Now what about money?' said Amber practically. 'For a start, you'll need expenses.'

Louise, as always, felt rather diffident about money, so she said, 'There's no need. We can discuss that side of it later, Lady Winterhaven.'

'Amber,' Lady Winterhaven reminded her. 'Very well, so long as you're happy about it.'

With Edgar's cheque, Louise knew she would have no trouble meeting her expenses getting to France, so she assured Amber that she was, 'Quite happy.'

They rang off after a few more exchanges, and Louise slumped back in Edgar's chair with a sigh. A smile spread across her face. What a turnabout! The last thing she had expected. She was still rather perplexed, and slightly uneasy about the whole business, but she could hardly have changed her mind when only a few hours ago she had expressed her willingness to take on the commission. It was only now, knowing that she was going after all, that she realised the full extent of her disappointment before.

Edgar came in, and at the sight of her, stopped in surprise.

'What's this? Wreathed in smiles! What did she offer, compensation?'

Louise shook her head. 'Apparently there was a misunderstanding. This Roland person had his wires crossed, so she says, and I'm to go after all.'

Edgar dragged her to her feet and whirled her around. 'But that's wonderful! Fantastic!' He kissed her heartily. 'My dear Louise, I'm delighted for you.'

Louise felt a bit lightheaded, from the wine at lunch and the unexpected turnaround of events. 'Edgar, put me down. You're making me dizzy!'

He set her, breathless, back on her feet, and held her face firmly but gently between his slender artistic hands. 'Now don't forget, take it easy, don't get in a dead funk, and remember I have faith in your ability even if you haven't much in yourself.'

'Noted!' said Louise.

'Good girl. Now, off you go and get yourself organised. Give me a call before you leave and we'll have dinner. Wait a minute . . . here's your cheque.' He took out his chequebook and wrote with a flourish, tore off the cheque and handed it to her. 'Now, run along. I've got masses to do and you've disrupted my day enough already!'

Louise decided to spend a night in Paris and drive down to the Château des Ormeaux the following day. The back of her small car was crammed with canvases, easel, paints and all the paraphernalia of her profession. In the boot was her suitcase, containing the few clothes she had that she hoped would be suitable for her stay at the château. Most of it was casual wear and working smocks, but she had included several more formal dresses. It was almost her complete wardrobe, she reflected, musing that everything would seem very cheap and meagre compared with Lady Winterhaven's elegant clothes.

She felt a little nervous every time she thought of living at the château with the family, but trying to imagine exactly what it would be like was impossible. She didn't even know how Roland Winterhaven fitted into the picture, and she was not exactly looking forward to seeing him again. She had deduced that he lived at the Château des Ormeaux too. Several times she wished she was not going, but then she would remember Edgar's words and steel herself. After all, deep down, she wanted to go.

It was a beautiful spring day when she set out from Paris, and the serene beauty of the countryside swept away her nerves and lifted her spirits sky high. There were trees in full bloom everywhere and amid the cherry, almond and plum, some of the other trees were putting on a haze of green.

It was quite a while since she had been to France, not since she had come to the Loire Valley with a painting group while she was still an art student. Paul had been among that crowd, and they had fallen in love . . .

The thought of Paul constantly arose at unexpected moments even now, and although her feelings for him had dimmed, the memories could still hurt. It had been wonderful to be in love. She recalled wistfully how blue the sky had seemed, how bright the colours, how broad the smiles on people's faces, how light her heart.

She swept the memories aside. She felt too light-hearted today to allow thoughts of Paul and being in love to spoil her mood. She hummed a tune happily as she drove farther and farther into château country, occasionally catching sight of towered and turreted and moated châteaux nestling amid the half bare trees, or flaunting themselves boldly from hilltops.

It was perfect countryside for an artist, she thought, resisting constant urges to park at the roadside and get out her paints to capture scenes. In the soft spring sunshine the landscape was gentle, its contours softened by a mauve haze, and the river, winding through green fields and between avenues of willow, alder and other greening trees, shone like curls of mauve satin ribbon. The grey slate roofs of villages and farmhouses seemed to merge into the haze and everywhere the stone farmhouses and bridges were mellow in the sun.

Louise stopped for lunch at Amboise. First she parked near the river across from the château, and there she did snatch a few minutes to sketch the scene. The rugged battlements thrust upwards from the far bank, violent history etched in every stone. The serene river flowed lazily beneath the bridge. A man fished from a small rowing boat, leaning back, his hat over his face, as still as though painted on the scene, and not a ripple stirred either boat or line. Louise did not linger too long because treacherously the scene began to remind her again of those halcyon days when she had been in love.

Restored after a meal of thick farmhouse soup, cheese and freshly baked warm bread, she set off again. As she headed away from the town, her nervousness crept back. She stopped once or twice to consult her map, got lost once and had to retrace her route, but eventually found the right road. She saw the château long before she reached it. Acres of vineyards flowed around it, a sea of rich brown newly ploughed earth with the buds barely showing on the long rippling rows of neatly pruned and tied vines. The château stood out vividly white against a backdrop of dark woods.

Louise drove through the entrance to the estate where its name was prominently displayed, and up a long drive between the vines. There was no justification for her growing trepidation, she kept telling herself. Who could be pleasanter and friendlier than Lady Winterhaven? It was just that she never could quite overcome her initial anxiety when confronted by something new or an unfamiliar situation.

As she approached the château, Louise saw that the vines did not sweep right up to the door as it had seemed from a distance. There were quite extensive grounds around the ancient house, with a lake some little distance away from it. Near the lake were several groups of elm trees, and it was from these, Louise supposed, that the château took its name.

The château itself suddenly loomed lofty and impressive above her, with towers and turrets and mullioned windows. Like a fairytale castle, she thought. It was not large, but to Louise it was both beautiful and awe-inspiring. As she turned in front of it and braked to a halt, she caught her breath. She had climbed higher than she had imagined, and the view of the surrounding countryside was a breathtaking panorama in the mellow afternoon light.

Pausing for a few moments as she got out of her car, Louise regarded the pile of ancient weathered and whitened stone that was to be her home for the next few weeks, and felt a mixture of thrill and apprehension.

'Better go and announce myself,' she muttered resolutely at last.

She walked swiftly up to the front door. Amber would tell her what to do with her car and where to take her luggage. She made a concerted effort to throw off the feeling of uneasiness that had followed her all the way. Everything would be all right as soon as she saw Amber Winterhaven again.

She pushed the bell beside the front door. It seemed somehow inappropriate. A large clanging bell, or rope, would have been more in keeping with the mediaeval atmosphere.

She waited impatiently. At first it seemed no one was coming, and her agitation increased. She couldn't have made a mistake, could she? No, of course not. This was definitely the Château des Ormeaux. It had said so at the entrance to the estate.

At last the door opened. A pretty French maid looked enquiringly out at Louise.

'*Bonjour*,' the maid murmured, and looked Louise over questioningly.

'I'm Louise Peterson,' said Louise quickly, and then in spite of her flustered feelings, she remembered a little school French. 'Louise Peterson,' she repeated. '*Je voudrais voir* Lady Winterhaven. *Elle m'attend.*'

The girl smiled. '*Oui! Oui!*' She held the door open wide. '*Entrez, s'il vous plaît, mademoiselle.*'

Louise tentatively walked into the vast entrance hall and looked around her. There was a staircase rising to another floor and doors leading off on either side. The stone floor was softened by rugs and the austere walls by pictures and tapestries.

The maid explained, 'Madame la Comtesse *n'est pas ici. Elle retournera bientôt.*'

Louise's heart sank a little. She had expected Amber to be there to greet her, and learning that she was out, even if expected back shortly, was a disappointment. Her French was not up to conversing in any detail with the maid, so she allowed the girl to lead her into a small sitting room in which a fire was burning. The maid said something rather too rapidly for Louise to understand, but she did catch the word *thé*, so guessed she was being asked if she would like some *tea*.

'*Oui, s'il vous plaît*,' she answered, and smiled. The maid smiled back, seemed satisfied, and having motioned Louise to, '*Asseyez-vous, je vous en prie, mademoiselle*,' she departed.

Louise chose a comfortable tapestry-covered chair not too near the fire and sat down. The sitting room was in sharp contrast to the vast hallway. It was small and intimate and looked like a family room, much lived in. There was a television set in one corner and a record player in another. There were books and magazines strewn about and several children's toys on a chaise-longue and under a coffee table.

Louise began to feel more relaxed in this homely atmosphere. She had not been there more than a few minutes when she heard the door open, and she turned from staring into the fire, expecting to see the maid bringing in tea. To her dismay the figure in the doorway was not the petite French girl, but the large forbidding frame of Roland Winterhaven. He looked as startled to see her as she was to see him.

He marched into the room, flinging the door to with a slam behind him. His eyes were dark with anger as well as incredulity.

'That is your car outside, I presume?' he said.

'Yes.' Louise's hands were trembling, and she clasped them tightly together in her lap.

The dark eyes locked with hers. 'May I enquire what you're doing here?'

Louise straightened her back as he continued to glower at her through the thick dark lashes that half hid his steely eyes. She must not let him intimidate her. Everything was perfectly all right; Amber had said so.

'I'm here at the request of Lady Winterhaven, to paint her children's portraits and also her husband's,' she stated defensively.

His frown deepened and his thick dark eyebrows almost met above his straight, almost classic nose. 'I believe I told you it was not convenient for you to come here at the moment,' he said, barely controlling his anger.

Louise was determined not to let him browbeat her this time. 'Lady Winterhaven telephoned me afterwards,' she said calmly, 'and she explained about the misunderstanding . . .'

'Misunderstanding?' he roared. 'What misunderstanding? There is no misunderstanding. Lady Winterhaven is not here, and I don't understand why *you* are, Miss Peterson.'

Louise flinched. She felt like a criminal under that accusing gaze. 'Not here?' she echoed. 'But surely I understood the maid to say she was out but would soon be back.' Had she gravely misunderstood, she wondered now, in her ignorance of the language?

He said emphatically, 'She is not expected back for some weeks. She's holidaying in England, as you know.'

Louise was utterly perplexed. 'But she telephoned me. She said it was all a mistake, and I was to come as planned.'

His eyes narrowed and his lips parted slightly. He caught his bottom lip on a top tooth thoughtfully, but before he could speak again the maid entered, and stopped in surprise.

'Monsieur Roland!' Clearly she had not expected to see him. She placed the tea tray on the table near Louise and looked apprehensively at him.

Roland Winterhaven immediately turned to her and rattled off something rapidly in French. The girl flinched, but she replied volubly. The exchange was much too fast for Louise to follow but she caught several words—*aujourd'hui*—*Madame la Comtesse*—*tous les enfants*—and then both of them looked at her, while fresh explanations poured from the maid's lips. Finally Roland Winterhaven said crisply, '*Bien. C'est tout, Marie.*'

The girl, with a speculative glance at Louise, scurried out. As the door closed behind her, Roland Winterhaven moved closer to Louise and stood looking down at her, his mouth twisted in an ironic smile. There was no amusement in the smile, only a grim determination. He said briskly, 'I'm very sorry, Miss Peterson, but you've again been put to quite unnecessary inconvenience. Your journey has been for nothing. I'm afraid Lady Winterhaven has acted rather impetuously, but the situation remains as before. It's quite impossible for you to remain here at the moment, and besides, another artist has been selected to paint Sir Peter's portrait. Lady Winterhaven misinformed you. Of course I shall reimburse you for any expenses you've incurred.'

His meaning was quite clear. He wanted her to leave now, right this minute. Louise was bewildered and not a little angry. She might be nervous of new situations, but she had plenty of spirit, especially when she felt she was being pushed around, as she did now. This was the second time he had peremptorily tried to get rid of her.

She stood up, but maintained her ground. 'I think I should wait to see Lady Winterhaven,' she said firmly, meeting his eyes boldly. She had no intention of being used like a football in one of their contests of will.

He made to take hold of her arm as he had before at the apartment in London, but she moved aside to avoid him. That placating gesture, she knew, was a pretence. He just wanted to march her off the premises.

He addressed her politely. 'Miss Peterson, I'm sorry this unfortunate situation has occurred, and in order to avoid any further unpleasantness, it would be best if you were to leave at once—preferably before Lady Winterhaven returns.'

'I was engaged by Lady Winterhaven,' said Louise bluntly. 'Why should I go just because you tell me to? Why are you being so difficult over it?'

His eyes sparked. 'That's none of your business,' he replied in a crushing tone.

'I suggest that it *is* my business,' Louise answered, surprised at her own asperity. But this man riled her as no one had ever done. 'I've evidently come all the way to France on a wild goose chase, in which case I feel I might at least be offered a plausible explanation. I understood that the redecorating could be postponed.'

To her satisfaction, he looked rather taken aback. Evidently he had expected her to acquiesce as meekly as she had back in London. Her stand surprised him.

After a moment he replied levelly, 'I've offered you adequate recompense for your inconvenience.'

'If you're trying to buy me off,' said Louise, incensed by his ruthless manner, and now the rather frank appraisal that his eyes were making of her, 'I'm afraid you won't succeed. This time I shall wait and see Lady Winterhaven. She asked me to come. I shall go only if she tells me to.'

She had a feeling that he would like to shake her and toss her out like a puppy that has fouled the carpet. However, he seemed to control the urge and said in a more conciliatory tone, 'I understand your annoyance and confusion, Miss Peterson, but it might help you to know that I control Lady Winterhaven's affairs, and my approval is necessary for all expenditure. If I refuse to approve, you will, I'm afraid, not be paid for your work.'

'I could sue!' blurted Louise.

He regarded her with disdain. 'You would be much more sensible to take on another commission. I understood from Lady Winterhaven that Mr Benson told her you're much in demand.'

Louise almost choked. Edgar, you idiot! she thought. She squared her shoulders and lifted her chin a little. She said in a firm even voice, 'I am not going until I've seen Lady Winterhaven. She must return soon, and perhaps then we can resolve the matter finally.'

He drew his lips together. 'You're a very stubborn young woman.'

He moved closer to her and instinctively Louise retreated. Something about him alarmed her. As he approached her again, and she again moved out of his way, she stumbled against a chair. He caught hold of her, steadied her, and then held her in a ferocious grip while he kissed her hard and brutally, almost squeezing the breath out of her.

For a moment Louise was so thunderstruck, she could do nothing to resist him except clench her teeth against his savagely seeking mouth. Her struggles were futile, he was too strong. When he finally released her, she sprang back, quivering with fury and badly shaken.

'How dare you!' she spat at him furiously.

'If you persist in defying me, I may do worse than that!' he said in a menacing tone. 'I'm rather partial to dark-haired beauties with strong wills and supple bodies!'

'You . . . you brute!' Louise breathed.

'I should go now,' he suggested smoothly, 'while you still have the chance.'

'Are you threatening me?' demanded Louise hotly.

'Are you suggesting that if I stay I run the risk of being—raped?'

He was laughing silently at her, she could see, mocking her cruelly with those dark unfathomable eyes. 'I'm sure I shouldn't be able to resist the temptation,' he declared casually.

'You'd never succeed!' retaliated Louise.

His eyes glinted, and in spite of herself she was disturbingly aware of his intense masculinity. He said slowly, 'I wouldn't bank on that.'

To Louise it was more of a challenge to dig her heels in than ever. She would show him that brute force did not always win.

'*I* would!' she announced in a firm clear voice.

Their eyes met and locked in battle. Neither would relent and look away. Louise knew that she was probably being dangerously foolish, and would regret her stubborn stand, but she could not back down now. She was determined to see it through, and discover what it was all about once and for all.

Fortunately, the moment was shattered by the voice of Amber Winterhaven, who burst breathlessly into the room.

'Louise . . .' Her smile of greeting faded and became a look of consternation as she saw Roland. '*Roland!* I thought you weren't going to be here for another week.' She coloured with embarrassment and her eyes faltered as they met Roland's steely gaze. She turned apologetically to Louise. 'I'm so sorry . . . I'd expected to be here when you arrived, but my car broke down on the way home from visiting a friend, and I had such a devil of a job getting the road patrol, and he took ages to get it started again, or I would have been back long ago.' She slid a defiant glance at Roland, smiling sweetly. 'Well, as you see, Roland, Miss Peterson is here after all.'

'Yes,' he said, 'she is.'

'I hope you're not going to be unpleasant and continue to argue about it,' said Amber, a glint of challenge in her eyes, 'because I'm determined she's going to stay.'

To Louise's amazement he accepted this rebellion without argument. He merely said, 'That's entirely up to Miss Peterson.'

And with a long searing look at Louise, that seemed to tear every stitch from her body as she stood there, leaving her naked to his gaze, he turned on his heel and walked from the room.

CHAPTER FOUR

AMBER WINTERHAVEN looked at Louise in blank astonishment.

'Pheww!' she exclaimed, as she threw herself down into the nearest chair and crossed her very elegant legs which were encased in expensive leather boots. She smoothed her camel-coloured suede skirt over her knees and twirled the gold chains which hung against a creamy wool sweater.

Louise was utterly speechless. She sank back into a chair too.

Amber went on, 'I can't believe it! The battle's won—and without firing another shot! I was all set for another flaming row.' She leaned forward. 'Is there any tea left? I'm parched.'

'I . . . I haven't had any yet,' said Louise, finding her voice.

Amber felt the teapot. 'It seems quite hot. I'll just call Marie to bring another cup.' She jumped up and pushed a bell for the maid, then she turned round, gave a little skip and began to laugh apologetically.

'My goodness, Louise, you must think us a very peculiar family!' She scrutinised Louise shrewdly. 'Roland must have got a hell of a shock finding you here. Was he angry? Did he try to send you away again?'

Louise gulped. She simply could not bring herself to tell Amber exactly what had happened. 'Er . . . he was a bit taken aback,' she conceded, adding quickly,

'I'm really rather confused. I . . . I feel sort of caught in the middle of something. Mr Winterhaven seems to feel very strongly about my being here.'

Amber sat down again and resting her elbows on the arms of the chair, joined her beringed fingers. She was still chuckling. 'I'm terribly sorry,' she said, 'I shouldn't laugh, but this has something of the quality of a farce, and I can't help seeing the absurdity of it! You see, I thought I'd foiled Roland perfectly.

'I knew it was useless arguing with him, so I pretended to give in, and then telephoned you to tell you it was all right. I knew he was going to Paris on business, and then attending some conference of *vignerons*, so I thought we'd be quite safe. By the time he came home, you would be here, and it would be a *fait accompli* and he'd have to put off the renovators. I don't know why he's so anxious to have things done, it isn't all that vital. It annoyed me that he was being so adamant about it.

'I certainly didn't reckon on him returning today of all days, and I would have to have trouble with the car! I went to visit a friend this morning, who persuaded me to stay for lunch. I left straight afterwards, knowing you were coming, and the car broke down. You can't imagine my frustration. I knew Marie would look after you, of course, but I didn't expect Roland!' She leaned forward, chuckling softly. 'You could have knocked me down with a feather when he said it was up to you . . .' She paused, looking quizzically at Louise. 'I'm not sure exactly what he meant by that remark, are you?'

Louise shrugged. Her uppermost instinct now was to turn and run, to tell Amber that she had changed her mind, but she knew Amber would try to dissuade her, and besides, there was the desire, growing stronger all the time, to show the arrogant Mr Winterhaven that he could not have everything his own way—not with her! She sympathised greatly with Amber if he always treated her plans in such an imperious manner.

'No . . .' she answered, in as level a voice as she could manage, 'I don't know what he meant. I haven't changed my mind.'

Amber sighed. 'Oh, it's just Roland being dour and cryptic and thoroughly infuriating, as usual. When he makes up his mind about something he hates being thwarted, although he's making rather an unnecessary fuss about this.'

Marie came in. Anticipating Amber's need, she had brought a second cup and saucer. She poured tea for them both and handed round the plate of almond biscuits.

When she had gone, Amber said, 'I'm sure you think Roland's behaviour quite extraordinary—and I confess I agree. I really don't know why he's making such an enormous issue over it. It almost seems as though he doesn't want anyone here, though I can't imagine why.' She laughed. 'Oh, dear, perhaps I can. Maybe he was planning to invite some luscious young lady here to stay and we've spoiled it!'

Louise murmured, 'Perhaps,' and thought it was highly likely. Roland had certainly seemed very anxious to be rid of her.

Amber went on, 'Well, whatever his plot, I'm afraid he'll have to put up with us now.' She waved a dismissive hand and shook her blonde hair back over her shoulders. She was stunningly attractive,

Louise thought, with a tinge of envy.

'You're probably wondering,' Amber said, 'why Roland lives here, and tries to bully me.'

'He did say he manages your affairs,' said Louise.

'Yes, he does. That was Peter's idea, and I don't object to it—I'm hopeless at money matters and I couldn't run the estate by myself . . . I'd better start at the beginning. I married Peter Winterhaven when I was very young—twenty years old. He was a good deal older, as you've probably guessed, since he's to be honoured for his heroism during the Second World War. We were very happy nonetheless, and his death was a great blow to me . . .' She paused and a look of sadness crossed her delicate features. Then she drew a deep breath. 'But life must go on . . . and there are the children to think of. Peter was married before, but had no children. Several years before we met he took Roland, who's his nephew, under his wing—a substitute son, you might as well say. Roland's own parents were both dead.

'Marrying again and having a family presented Peter with something of a problem, and he solved it in the fairest way he could. He had long treated Roland as his son, so he left the estate to him, with the proviso that I and the children must be allowed to live here, and must be provided for, myself until I die or marry, the children until they come of age and inherit their capital. It's a complicated will and I won't go into it more than that, but Roland controls the purse strings, as you might say, and a very strict controller he is.' She grimaced before going on, 'It's for our own good and I know he's right, that inflation is eating into our investments, and that I can't afford to splash out on every whim that takes my fancy . . .'

She chuckled. 'He regarded you as a whim—or perhaps that was just an excuse to stop you coming.'

'You mean he doesn't think you can afford me,' said Louise, amused.

Amber laughed. 'I told him if he was going to be mean about it, Mother would pay! I'm quite determined to have the portraits done now, and I want you to do them. I don't want to postpone the idea and then find you're not available. The children won't be young for ever and I want to remember them the way they are right now. Oh, I've got heaps of photographs, but that's not the same. Good paintings last for ever, Peter used to say. He was a collector, Louise, and had a fine collection of Impressionist and post-Impressionist works. Mostly lesser-known names, although there were a couple of small Manets and a fine Sisley. General d'Arbrisseau has them now. He's a neighbour of ours.'

Louise, surprised, said, 'Your husband sold them?'

Amber nodded. 'He wanted to finance a home for war veterans at Juan-les-Pins, and selling the pictures was the only way to raise the money. He persuaded quite a few people to contribute, but the General, although he's quite rich, refused. He's a charming but rather mean man.' She pursed her lips. 'He doesn't know a lot about art, and he envied Peter's collection, so he offered to buy it.' She shrugged. 'Peter hated parting with the pictures. They were his pride and joy because he collected every one himself after the war, going to sales, and tracking different ones down in the oddest places, but in the end he capitulated and sold them so he could make the home a reality.' She smiled reminiscently. 'That was Peter.'

'He must have been a wonderful man,' commented Louise.

Amber sipped her tea. 'He was.' She sighed deeply. 'He even said he hoped I would marry Roland if anything happened to him.'

Louise was startled. 'Marry Roland?'

'Peter was a realist. I'm only a year or two older than Roland, and if we married it would tidy everything up nicely, wouldn't it?' She chuckled. 'But it wouldn't stop him bullying me! Roland is very masterful, a man who expects and usually gets everything his own way. Oh, he's usually right, I give him that, and he manages the estate far better, I have to confess, than even Peter did. He's ruthlessly efficient, and he's exceedingly good to me and the children. It's just that sometimes I feel I have to dig my heels in and assert my independence—like now!' She looked candidly at Louise. 'I suppose I could have agreed to postponing your coming and made a future arrangement with you on the spot since the decorators won't be here for long, but Roland could have given in too just as easily . . .'

'You two are very forceful personalities,' said Louise. 'Do you think that will make for a harmonious marriage?' She hoped she wasn't being too personal, even though Amber was being quite frank.

Amber did not seem to mind. She smiled at Louise, her blue eyes twinkling. 'He's very attractive, don't you think? Very masculine.'

Louise was caught unawares, and felt her colour immediately rising. 'Er . . . yes, I suppose so.'

Amber was delighted. 'Come, admit it, he has a devastating way of looking at a woman through those ridiculously thick lashes of his that makes your insides feel they've just been through a blender. It isn't love, just good old-fashioned sex appeal. Roland is one of the sexiest men I know ... what about you?'

Her new employer's forthrightness continued to startle Louise. 'I don't know many men,' she answered, all the time thinking of the cataclysmic kiss she had experienced in this very room only minutes ago. Roland was a polished performer, she was in no doubt about that.

'What about Edgar?' asked Amber. 'Edgar's rather a dishy person, isn't he?'

'He's been very good to me,' hedged Louise. 'Yes, I suppose he is quite dishy.'

Amber laughed. 'I see you prefer not to commit yourself too directly. Good for you. It doesn't do to wear your heart on your sleeve.' She paused and became serious. 'I'm sorry, I'd forgotten for a moment, you mentioned you'd lost your fiancé?'

'Yes. He was killed in a motorcycle accident.'

Amber's face showed sympathetic pain. 'How dreadful for you! I know what it must have been like. Peter crashed his car. He was racing ... something he shouldn't have been doing at his age, but at least he died doing something he enjoyed.' She sighed deeply. 'But for the one who's left it's as though someone has come along and blasted a thumping great hole in your life, one you fear will never be filled.'

'It's like that exactly,' agreed Louise, leaning forward eagerly. 'I feel sometimes that the part of me that feels is dead, too ...' She stopped. Already that was a lie, she thought. Only minutes ago she had experienced an involuntary resurrection of feelings she had thought dead and buried with Paul. That a man like Roland Winterhaven should have been responsible made her feel ashamed.

Amber said, 'It isn't as if you still grieve . . . there's just a void.'

'Edgar says I'm still carrying a torch for Paul,' said Louise, encouraged by Amber's sympathetic understanding. 'But it isn't even that. I don't believe you can go on loving someone who isn't there, because love isn't a one-way thing, is it?' She stopped short again, afraid she had presumed, suggesting something Amber might not share.

But it was not so. 'My feelings exactly,' said Amber. 'I loved Peter very much, even though he was old enough to be my father. Perhaps that was why; my own father had always been too busy making money to have time for his children. I was never unfaithful to Peter, I never once looked at a younger man, but now the truth is I'm ready to fall in love again, and I feel guilty about it.'

With Roland? Louise wondered. Amber had sidestepped her question earlier, probably because she was not sure of her feelings yet, and because of her sense of guilt. Perhaps the real reason for Amber's insisting on returning to the château was her suspicion that Roland wanted to entertain another woman. Perhaps she was jealous and wanted to frustrate it? These and other intriguing thoughts slid around in her mind as she said, 'I'd like to know as much about your husband as possible if I'm to paint his portrait, especially, of course, about his wartime activities.'

Amber jerked back from the reverie she seemed to have drifted into. 'Yes, of course. I'll give you the proofs of his biography to read later. But briefly, now, Peter wasn't French, as you might have deduced from the name, but he was half French. His father was Anglo-German and his mother was French. She inherited the estate from her parents. Peter grew up speaking not only English—he went to school in England—but French and German as well, fluently.

'During the war he organised a local cell of the Resistance, and later was in charge of a whole area. He wouldn't often talk about it, but when he did he made it sound merely daredevil and exciting. They used to hide airmen and escaped prisoners in the château. Hundreds got away because of them. Peter always brushed off any talk of heroism as though it was no more than a Boy Scout's good deed. He had a tremendous lust for life, my husband, and was quite fearless. He was a fencing champion before the war, and also a brilliant chemist. He contributed some quite significant advances to the chemistry of wine-making. He was dedicated to helping ex-Resistance men, but not only them. The causes he gave time and money to were legion.'

'But he must have been exceedingly modest,' remarked Louise, 'since he refused to be honoured in his own lifetime.'

'He didn't want to be honoured at all. Strange, because he was a total extrovert. But he hated publicity. I couldn't even persuade him to sit for a portrait, so I'm afraid you'll have to work entirely from photographs. Do you mind?'

Suddenly remembering, Louise answered carefully, 'I understood from Mr Winterhaven that a local artist has already been chosen to paint the portrait.'

Amber's features set in a stubborn expression. 'No, that isn't so. The mayor and his cronies have one in mind, but I don't like his work. It's flat and lifeless. They have to have my approval, so I don't think there'll be any problems. Roland said that to try and put you off, I'm sure.' Suddenly she jumped up. 'What are we doing, sitting here gossiping, when you must be so tired driving all that way? I'm so thoughtless—but I am enjoying talking to you, Louise. You're going to be very good for me. We're on the same wavelength, I feel sure.'

As they went towards the door, Louise said, 'I stayed the night in Paris and drove down very leisurely today. I had lunch in Amboise and did a bit of sketching near the castle.'

'Did you? I love Amboise,' enthused Amber. 'And Blois. They're two of my favourite local places. Have you been to Le Clos-Lucé?'

'No . . . where is that?'

'Amboise. It's the house where Leonardo da Vinci lived in his later years. There's a marvellous exhibition of maquettes there, models made to scale from his mechanical drawings. There's even his version of an aeroplane! You must go there one day.'

'I mustn't forget I'm here to work,' Louise reminded her with a smile.

Amber brushed the remark aside. 'Come on, let's see about your room and your luggage.' She rang for Marie and when the girl appeared, spoke rapidly to her in French.

'Henri will carry your luggage up,' said Amber, turning back to Louise, 'and he'll put your car away. I'll take you straight up to your room. It's all ready for you.'

'My painting gear is in the back of the car,' said Louise. 'I'd like to see to that myself. Otherwise, there's just one suitcase in the boot.'

'Henri will love you!' declared Amber, as they went out of the room. She went on, 'I've had a room in the West Tower cleared for you as a studio. It has windows all round and I thought it would be most suitable, but if you prefer somewhere else, please tell me. You can put all your paraphernalia in there.'

An elderly man with almost white hair, and a slight stoop, came into the hall. A strong smell of French cigarettes came with him.

'Ah, Henri,' said Amber, and spoke to him in French. Then she turned to Louise, and introduced her.

'Henri Leveque is his name and he's rather deaf,' she whispered to Louise. 'But I suspect he can lip-read!'

'*Bonjour*, Monsieur Leveque,' said Louise slowly and distinctly.

'*Enchanté, mademoiselle*,' he replied, and bowed slightly.

'He fought with Peter in the Resistance,' explained Amber later as, after first taking her up to the tower, she was showing Louise to her bedroom. 'He would have done anything for Peter, even died for him.'

She threw open the door of Louise's room and Louise walked in. It was a large chamber, half panelled, and comfortably and colourfully furnished.

'I hope you'll be comfortable,' said Amber. 'Your bathroom is over there.' She pointed to a door on the far side, and seeing Louise's pleased surprise, 'Peter liked the mediaeval atmosphere of the château to be preserved, but he didn't approve of mediaeval plumbing! Now, I'll leave you to wash and change and have a rest if you wish. Come down whenever you are ready. The children are dying to see you again. They're out this afternoon with their nanny,

Philippa Best, whom you'll meet later. Otherwise they would have been in your hair already.'

When Amber had gone Louise took a fresh look at her surroundings, and liked what she saw. The room was bright and cheerful, and crossing to look out of the stone-mullioned window she found she had a breathtaking view down over the lake into the misty distance. Dusk was falling, and the brilliant sunset flaming across the sky was in startling contrast to the dark grey landscape. The river in the distance reflected the blazing sky and flowed like molten gold.

Louise, to her own surprise, did not feel in the least tired. She freshened up under the shower in the green and gold bathroom, and then debated what to wear for the evening. In the end she chose the deep cherry red wool dress with long fitted sleeves, a softly folded neckline and full skirt, because the colour, she felt, would give her the courage she needed to face Roland Winterhaven again.

She brushed her dark hair and tucked it behind her ears, using silver-edged combs to keep it there. She wore the silver filigree earrings Paul had given her, and the matching bracelet, her only good jewellery and the only pieces she had brought with her. It was almost seven o'clock by then, so hoping she would not be too late to see the children, she hurried downstairs.

There was no one about as she stood hesitantly in the hall, wondering what to do. After a moment or two's consideration she decided to see if there was anyone in the small sitting room where she had earlier had tea with Amber. She approached it nervously. Her dramatic interview with Roland Winterhaven was still engraved deeply on her mind.

She was about to open the door when Marie, the maid, appeared, and spoke to her. Louise smiled and held out her hands helplessly. '*Je ne vous comprends pas*, Marie.'

Marie gave a shrug. She walked towards a door on the other side of the hall and opened it, motioning Louise to enter. Louise did so and found herself in a large drawing room which at first she thought was empty, but as her eyes slowly roved round the room, taking in the red velvet, the tapestries, the chandeliers, the richly patterned deep-pile carpet, they came to rest at last on the figure standing near the fire which burned cheerfully in the huge grate. The curtains were drawn and the light from the standard lamps had left him in part shadow, so that in his dark suit he was not immediately noticeable.

Louise's eyes finally reached his, and for a moment she knew a tremendous urge to turn and run. It was the effect he wanted to have on her, she felt sure, so she resisted it with all her might, and walked further into the room, wishing he was not alone, and that someone would soon come and join them.

He said, a trifle irascibly, 'Come in, come in.'

'Good evening, Mr Winterhaven,' Louise murmured politely.

'*Bonsoir, mademoiselle*,' he answered with a slightly mocking bow. 'Please call me Roland. Amber has told me you and she have already agreed to first names.'

Louise nodded. 'Thank you.'

'You would care for something to drink?' He was being exaggeratedly polite, and Louise wished he would not look at her quite so intently.

'A dry sherry would be nice,' she said, immediately

feeling it had been a rather unsophisticated choice, and wishing she had chosen something more regional.

However, he did not question her choice but crossed to a cocktail cabinet and poured out the drink. As he handed it to her he said, sweeping his dark compelling eyes over her in a thoroughly disconcerting manner, 'What a charming dress. And red is such a provocative colour!'

Louise sensed that he was playing with her, like a cat with a mouse, and enjoying her discomfort. He was not going to forgive her readily for standing up to him and causing his plans to go awry. Momentarily, she felt a pang of guilt. Perhaps he had every right to want a little privacy. If she hadn't been so stubborn, Amber might have capitulated and returned to England as he wished. Louise wondered if his real reason for not wanting them there was a woman. In spite of herself she was intrigued to know what kind of woman Roland Winterhaven would have an affair with.

'If it provokes you,' she answered coolly, 'I apologise, but I have a limited wardrobe and shall have to wear it quite often.'

He laughed softly. 'And you know it suits you, naturally!' He raised his glass which he had replenished, in a mocking toast. '*A votre santé* . . . and your stay here, be it short . . . or long!' He drank almost the whole of his drink in one draught.

Louise sipped her sherry and determined not to let him unnerve her. She must take special care, she reminded herself, to avoid being alone with him, not even in such innocuous circumstances as now. It was, she thought wryly, going to be a difficult commission, thanks to Roland Winterhaven's antagonism.

To her relief the door opened and Amber breezed in, preceded by the three older children. She was carrying the baby, Melissa. There ensued a lively few minutes while the children enthusiastically renewed their acquaintance with Louise, she was introduced to the baby and given Melissa to hold.

Roland meanwhile stood a little aloof from the scene, but when Louise inadvertently glanced in his direction, she found him looking at her speculatively and with a half smile on his lips as though he was enjoying a private joke. She shivered involuntarily. She had a strong feeling that he had not yet given up his determination to get rid of her.

'Now, children,' said Amber at last, 'I think you've bothered Miss Peterson quite enough. It's time you went to bed. Where's Pippy?' A young woman chose that moment to come in. It was the girl Louise had briefly glimpsed at the apartment in London. Amber said, 'Oh, good, there you are, Philippa. Come and meet Louise.'

Philippa Best looked Louise over with an appraising eye, but her greeting was warm and her smile friendly. She shepherded the children out and lifted Melissa from Louise's arms.

As she went Amber said, 'She's a treasure. You'll have more chance to chat to her at dinner—if she can settle those monsters in time!' She glanced at Roland, with a trace of anxiety still in her face, Louise thought. Perhaps she too thought he had not played all his cards yet. 'What brought you home so early? I thought the conference was for a whole week.'

'It is.' He spoke as he crossed to the cabinet and poured her a drink, knowing without asking apparently what she would have. 'I just got bored, that's all. I'd heard it all before. Nothing new.'

Amber raised her glass and slid a sly wink in Louise's direction. 'Well, here's to us—and the future.'

For the next few minutes the conversation was almost exclusively between Amber and Louise. Roland remained aloof and taciturn, leaning on the big carved stone mantelpiece, throwing another piece of wood on the fire, and solicitously refilling their glasses. Louise felt uneasily conscious of his eyes on her most of the time, even if they were not, and she was glad when Marie came in to say that dinner was ready.

Louise was prepared for the same constraint over the meal, but Philippa's presence helped to enliven it, and even Roland became a shade more talkative.

Once Amber said, 'I was telling Louise about Peter's art collection, Roland. I'm sure she would like to see the pictures. When are the d'Arbrisseaux due back, do you know?'

'Not for another few weeks,' he answered.

'Chantal too?' enquired Amber, with an expression that made Louise wonder if there was more behind the remark than there appeared.

'I presume so,' said Roland.

'Have you heard from her?' asked Amber casually.

'A postcard,' he said. 'And one letter. She's having a great time, naturally.'

Amber gave a silvery laugh and looked at Philippa and Louise.

'Chantal d'Arbrisseau is madly in love with Roland. She's only a child—eighteen—but very beautiful, very striking . . .' She gave Roland a rather arch look. 'But whether Roland is in love with her is another of his dark secrets.'

Roland said nothing. Yes, he would be a secretive man, thought Louise. He would give nothing away of his real feelings. Nothing would show in that handsome arrogant face that he did not want to show.

Later, after coffee in the drawing room, Philippa excused herself, so Louise did likewise, although pressed to stay by Amber. She said she wanted to slip up to the tower room to set out her art materials, which was true, although her real reason was to escape the discomfort of continually meeting Roland's gaze.

There were winding stairs which she ran up lightly to the narrow corridor which led to the tower room. She pushed open the big oak door of the West Tower room, looked around, and drew a deep breath. A studio in a château! The novelty of her surroundings still left her bemused.

She spent a little time setting up her easel and arranging her paints and brushes and sorting out the canvases she had brought. Then she idly turned over the leaves of a sketch pad and made a few lightning sketches from memory of the children's faces, in an effort to capture some of the liveliness she had observed in them this evening before dinner. All at once she found herself sketching a more sombre countenance, a man with a widow's peak of dark waving hair, lush dark lashes and a square uncompromising chin.

Annoyed with herself, she tore it out and ripped it up, then closed her sketchbook. Suddenly she felt tired. She took one last look around her eyrie, as she had begun to think of it. It was bare except for her painting materials, a small divan and a couple of chairs, but to her it was an excitingly attractive workplace and she could hardly wait to begin. She turned out the light and as she was closing the door behind her, she realised that the light was now off on the stairs. The corridor was in total darkness, except for a glimmer of light from a window at the far end.

As she stood waiting for her eyes to become more accustomed to the darkness before feeling her way along the corridor, a hand clamped firmly on her arm and Roland's voice rasped, 'Don't bother to scream. No on will hear you, the walls are two foot thick.'

The scream that had risen to her lips died, and she felt the door fall open behind her and then she was being pushed inside. This galvanised her into summoning all her strength to wrench herself out of his grasp. Free, she raced along the corridor in the dark, bumping against the wall, but she had gone only a few paces before he caught her, picked her up and flung her unceremoniously over his shoulder. He marched back to the studio with her ineffectually pummelling his back with her fists, and gasping with fury, while her heart beat wildly in panic.

CHAPTER FIVE

Hot tears of rage and humiliation stung Louise's eyes, but there was nothing she could do but keep up her futile battering on his solid implacable form during the seconds that seemed like years before he strode into the studio and slammed the stout wooden door behind him. She felt utterly foolish dangling over his shoulder like a rag doll, flaying her arms about while he held her in an iron grip behind the knees. There could be nothing more guaranteed to banish every shred of dignity than being carried in this crude fashion.

Roland switched on the light, and then with a heave tipped her forward so that she slid down on to her feet. Her caught her under the arms to steady her as her feet hit the stone floor. The blood which had rushed to her head before now began to subside, but her hair still hung in a tangle over her face. She was breathless with effort and fury, and now that the first shock was over, sheer terror. As she lifted a hand to part her hair, shaking it back from her face, her eyes met his, and his searing gaze left her only too unhappily sure of his intent.

But despite this, the fury he had aroused would not let her give in and agree to leave, even though that, she knew, would be by far the most sensible thing to do. With a sudden tremendous surge of energy she did not know she had left, she broke away from him and darted across the room, knowing she was gaining only temporary freedom, but like a captured animal, obeying a primitive instinct for survival. Frantically she looked around for something with which to fend him off, but there was nothing near her, not even a chair.

Roland did not move but watched her, a grim smile on his lips and, she thought, thoroughly enjoying her panic. Desperately she glanced around the room again, but he barred the way to the door and the windows were too small and too high off the ground to afford a means of escape. She was trapped very effectively, and it was her own fault, she recalled ruefully, for saying she was coming up here in his hearing. What a golden opportunity she had given him to carry out his threat!

'If you think you can drive me away with this disgusting kind of behaviour,' she said with a show of bravado she did not feel, 'then you're wrong. The more you torment me, the more determined I shall be to stay. Now, if you'll kindly stand aside, I should like to go to my room unmolested.'

His eyebrows rose. 'Indeed? I was not aware that you were in a position to dictate terms.' His smile twisted mockingly, giving his handsome features almost a satanic look, Louise thought.

She tried to tell herself that he was only trying to intimidate her, that he meant her no real harm, and yet the rapid beating of her heart showed she was unconvinced.

She said impatiently, 'This charade is quite ridiculous. What right have you to ride roughshod over Amber? Or me? If this is the only way you can exercise your will over people, then you can't be much of a man!'

He strode towards her and she flinched as she

waited for him to grab her. She knew she had gone too far with that last remark. He intended to show her how wrong she was. He stood close to her but did not touch her. Her legs would not move to take her away from him. Her will seemed vanquished by his.

He said, with perhaps a trace of reluctant admiration, 'You're quite a little spitfire underneath that self-effacing exterior, aren't you?'

'And you're a monster!' she retorted.

'Monster?' He seemed to find the description amusing. He studied her for a moment but still did not touch her. Then he said in a quieter tone, folding his arms and relaxing his stance a little, 'If I told you that there is a special reason for wanting you to leave the château and for Amber to continue her holiday in England, a very important reason that affects the happiness of a number of people, including her, would you co-operate?'

Louise was taken aback at this unexpected approach, but suspicious. 'So the renovating was a blind?'

'Not entirely. There are various things that need to be done. They would be seen to be done.'

'You don't want Amber to know the real reason,' Louise said.

'No.'

'Why not?' Louise was convinced now that Amber's suspicions of another woman were the right ones.

'I'm afraid I can't tell you,' said Roland.

'After the cock-and-bull stories you've told me so far,' Louise said coldly, 'you can hardly expect me to accept something on trust.'

'It's a very delicate situation . . .'

'Situations with women often are,' Louise interrupted bluntly.

He looked taken aback, as well he might, she thought. 'I'm not stupid,' she said, 'and neither is Amber. I think you'd better just postpone your assignation, or make other arrangements.'

'There is no assignation,' he said, but Louise felt sure he was lying. He went on, 'If you leave, Amber can be persuaded to go too. You can come back another time. I'll make sure it's arranged.'

'No,' said Louise, knowing her refusal boded ill for her. 'I'm not going. What excuse can I give to Amber now? Do I tell her you tried to rape me?'

'I haven't . . .'

'Not yet!'

A low chuckle broke from his lips. 'And if I do, perhaps you'll tell her not only that I tried but that you . . .'

'You're hateful!' exploded Louise, caught between fear of him and determination not to let him win by physical or other means.

'And you're a very obstinate young woman!'

She gritted her teeth. 'I suppose you thought I'd run at the first hint of violence. Well, you're wrong. I'm not going to sneak away in the middle of the night, which is what you'd like me to do, isn't it? The commission means a lot to me, and I don't intend to lose it, because in spite of what you said before, Amber wouldn't ask me back if I ran out on her, and I'm not going to lie to her, just because you've got some mysterious reason you won't reveal. I don't believe you anyway. Maybe there isn't any assignation, maybe you're just pigheaded and arro-

gant because you can't get your own way.' She clen-
ched her fists at her side and spat out, 'And believe
me, I won't make it easy for you!'

He chuckled. It was the kind of amusement that
should have sent a shiver of revulsion through her,
but to her chagrin she acknowledged it as attractive,
and in fact, despite hating him, she could not escape
the knowledge that he *was* attractive—dangerously
so, and in a brutal kind of way.

'No, I can see that!' he drawled, his eyes sliding
over her, 'Although I wonder . . . perhaps the prospect does please you . . .'

This second insinuation made Louise flare like a
match struck. She took one step towards him and
brought her hand up so swiftly he was unaware of
the movement until her palm flashed stingingly
across his cheek. The force caused his head to jerk to
one side and he was momentarily thrown off balance.
As he straightened up, Louise involuntarily stepped
back a pace, eyeing him warily.

Her reaction had been instinctive, and she knew
that antagonising him in this way was likely to prove
her downfall. He would want to punish her now,
even if he had been inclined to relent and resort to
persuasion before. She watched mesmerised as he
touched the already reddening patch on his cheek,
and her heart was pounding hard enough to burst out
of her ribcage.

'You little devil!' he breathed, the light of battle
kindling in his eyes. 'I've a good mind to teach you
the lesson of your life!'

'Why? Because *you* insulted *me*?' she retorted hotly.

He did not answer or move, but watched her with
smouldering eyes. His hand dropped to his side and,

to her immense surprise he said, 'For one so small and inoffensive-looking, you pack quite a punch!' He laughed. 'It seems I've met my match.' Then his expression hardened again. 'Very well, stay. Fortunately for you, your conscience will not be troubled for the rest of your life by the outcome, because you won't even know what you've done.'

With one last raking look, he turned and strode out of the studio. Louise remained rooted to the floor, unable to believe he had gone, as the reverberations of the slamming door echoed round the chamber, and without any further violence. His cryptic words rang in her ears, and despite her triumph, a faint uneasiness stirred in her. What had he meant? Swiftly she dismissed the feeling. He was merely trying to scare her psychologically now, since force had failed.

Slowly and warily, she crossed the chamber to the door, opened it and looked into the corridor. It was empty and the light was on. She closed the studio door and ran quickly downstairs to her bedroom. Her legs felt weak, as though she had run ten miles, and she all but collapsed on to her bed. The past half hour flashed across her mind again like some dreadful nightmare. It was difficult to believe it had happened.

In spite of her traumatic experience, Louise slept soundly that night, so exhausted was she both physically and mentally. She did not even dream. She was awakened by a maid drawing the curtains back and opening the shutters. It was not Marie but another girl who smiled at Louise as she surfaced reluctantly from the warmth of the feather quilt, and half sat up.

'*Bonjour, mademoiselle,*' said the girl cheerfully, adding, '*Je m'appelle* Céleste.'

'*Oh . . . bonjour*, Céleste,' answered Louise, yawning. '*Quelle heure est-il?*'

'*Il est huit heures*,' replied the maid, smiling.

Eight o'clock! Louise was appalled at having overslept. She was usually up much earlier than this.

Céleste enquired, '*Vous voudrez prendre le petit déjeuner dans votre chambre, mademoiselle?*'

'*Oui, s'il vous plaît*,' answered Louise, feeling pleased with herself for understanding that Céleste was asking if she would like breakfast in her room.

However, Céleste then rattled off a stream of French which left her floundering.

'Céleste!' Louise protested with a laugh, '*Je ne vous comprends pas!*'

Céleste looked surprised. Evidently she had assumed Louise spoke her language fluently. The maid smiled. '*Eh bien!*' she added in careful English, 'I speak a little English. I have been in England sometimes with Madame.'

'Good . . . *très bon* . . . *très bien* . . .' said Louise, stammering over the words. 'Then we will speak a little of both—slowly, shall we?'

Céleste laughed. '*Certainement!*'

Louise said, 'Céleste, is it usual to have breakfast in bed? I don't want to cause any bother.'

'*Oui* . . . oh, yes, yes,' Céleste assured her. 'Only Monsieur Roland does not.' She made a wry face. 'He is up before everyone else, even before the servants arrive!'

'He must work hard on the estate,' commented Louise.

'All the time,' Céleste replied, with admiration sparkling in her brown eyes.

While she went to fetch Louise's breakfast, Louise lay languidly in bed staring at the decoratively

moulded plaster ceiling, and as slowly last night came
back to her, vividly, she shuddered. Then she smiled,
involuntarily. She felt convinced now that her panic
had been unnecessary, that Roland had never intended to carry out his threat. He had merely hoped to
frighten her away. Her stand had nonplussed him,
and instead of forcing the issue, he had given in.
Perhaps he was not such a dreadful ogre after all.
She half regretted slapping his face, but he had certainly deserved it!

When Céleste returned with a tray, Louise discovered, as the aroma of freshly baked croissants and
rich flavoursome coffee drifted in with her, that she
was ravenously hungry. Céleste lingered to chat, and
Louise learned that she and Marie and the house-
keeper-cook were the only staff at the château apart
from a daily cleaning woman and old Henri Leveque.
Only Henri actually lived in; the others came in daily
from the village. Céleste was full of praise for both
Amber and Roland. She would not like to work for
anyone else, she said, adding confidingly, 'I 'ope they
will get married soon. That would be nice!' She
added with a touch of asperity, 'I do not like that
Chantal d'Arbrisseau. She is silly and vain and knows
nothing. If he marries her I shall leave!'

'Perhaps he loves her,' suggested Louise absently,
as she buttered a croissant.

Céleste stood with her hands on her hips. 'No. He
loves Madame. He has always loved her. Everyone
knows that. But she . . . she is faithful to Monsieur le
Comte.' She sighed romantically. 'It is a pity, but
perhaps one day she will change. I 'ope for it.'

Then, glancing at her watch, she made a face and
scuttled out, leaving Louise to finish her breakfast

alone and wonder whether Roland was aware yet that Amber was changing.

When Céleste returned for the tray some little time later, Louise was showered and dressed in tan slacks and an orange sweater. Céleste delivered a message from Amber to say that Louise would find her in the garden if she would like to come down later, but she was not to hurry and to remember that she was on holiday.

Louise tied her hair back with an orange ribbon and applied a light touch of make-up to her rather pale face. Her features, she decided, betrayed the ordeal she had been subjected to last night. She resolved to start filling her sketchbook today, so she went up to the tower to fetch it, feeling all the way a tingling sensation as she remembered what had occurred there last night.

Roland Winterhaven's presence seemed still to surround her, and she was shaking inside as she entered the studio and fumbled in her satchel for her sketchbook and pencils. She would do some wash drawings later, she decided, but for a start she wanted simply to capture a few angles, different poses and expressions, to get the feel of her subjects before she decided exactly how to pose them. It would make the sittings a lot easier if she knew exactly how she wanted to paint them from the start.

Before leaving the room she stood for a moment in the middle of the floor, and half closing her eyes, she could almost see herself and Roland as they had been last night, in direct and violent confrontation. She trembled as she recalled the way she had stood up to him, astonished still that she had had the nerve. But overriding this was a vague feeling of uneasiness again. How could her conscience be troubled? Had that remark been just a final attempt to unnerve her? Yes, she was certain it had been. She turned and walked resolutely from the room. If there really was a good solid reason for her to leave, he would surely have told her.

Louise, on going out into the garden, was surprised to find Amber, not idling away in a deck chair or even strolling among the flower beds, but actually digging one of them. Amber Winterhaven was dressed in a sweater and jeans and gumboots, with a scarf tied around her hair, and she was attacking the earth energetically with a spade. Melissa was parked in her pram nearby and Angela was at the edge of the garden bed, clad like her mother, and digging with a toy spade.

Amber stopped digging when she saw Louise. 'Hello there! How are you this morning, Louise? Did you sleep well?' She stuck the spade in the ground and walked over to join her.

'I slept very soundly,' admitted Louise, 'too soundly, I'm afraid. I don't usually get up so late.'

Amber dismissed her apology. 'You're on holiday. Edgar said you needed a break, so sleep in as often as you like. You had a tiring day yesterday, in any case.'

'Edgar always fusses,' said Louise guiltily. She actually felt wonderfully refreshed this morning. She asked, 'What are you going to plant here?'

'Marigolds, petunias . . . oh, and a few other things. Henri's got it all worked out,' said Amber. She added, 'Actually, my special forte is the vegetable garden. I've got cabbages, broccoli, runner beans in summer, lettuces, asparagus, and some excellent raspberry canes and redcurrant bushes. Come, I'll show you. I'm very proud of my garden.' She grinned engagingly. 'Roland thinks it's only an affectation, I'm sure—he thinks I'm really a flibbertigibert and spendthrift, but I'm not as feckless as he makes out.'

She showed Louise over the whole of the château gardens that morning and when they were walking beside the lake, she suddenly noticed that Louise was carrying her sketchbook.

'I see you mean to start work straight away,' she remarked.

'I thought I might make a few sketches just to get the feel of things,' said Louise diffidently.

'I suppose that's a good idea. Well, you do whatever you wish, Louise. Go anywhere you like. You'll find the children playing around somewhere, I expect. Selena and Simon are probably riding, and . . .' she broke into laughter suddenly, 'Angela's probably still digging that flower bed! I'd better get back and see what she's up to, and Melissa.'

'I'll just wander,' said Louise. 'It's a perfect morning and I'd like to absorb the atmosphere.' She took a deep breath. 'Isn't the air wonderful here?'

Amber agreed. 'I confess, though, loving it here as I do, I still like to go back to England sometimes. It's my first home and of course Mother likes to see us from time to time.' She made a wry face and confided, 'But the children wear her out a bit. I think she was quite relieved when I decided to come home early, though she'd never have said so.'

'Well, I hope I'll be able to justify your curtailing your holiday,' said Louise.

'Ah, that reminds me,' said Amber. 'I must make

an appointment for us to see the mayor to discuss Peter's portrait. You can see where it's to hang, decide on the size, and discuss anything else you need to with them.' She eyed Louise directly. 'And don't be diffident about your fee. They'll respect you more if you're not too cheap!' She added, 'I think we'll get it over as soon as possible, perhaps tomorrow if I can arrange it.'

Louise nodded. She felt anxious about the project, but as Amber was determined she should paint the portrait of her husband, she could not refuse. It worried her, however. So far everything she had heard about Peter Winterhaven seemed to indicate that he was little short of a saint, and Louise had the uneasy feeling that it would be difficult to paint a saint— especially since she was unable to see him in the flesh and form her own conclusions.

However, she put the difficulty from her mind as she wandered around the château grounds, feeling still rather like a little girl in a dream world, and still half afraid she might suddenly wake up in her flat in London. She paused often to make lightning sketches of background, and later, after the children had discovered her, of them as they played around her. She even sketched Amber wielding her spade, although Amber was unaware of this.

Once she was sitting on a low balustrade around the terrace across the front of the château, drawing with deep concentration the children who were playing with a tennis racquet and ball on the lawn a short distance away, when a shadow fell across her page. She glanced up and found Roland looking down at her. It was the first time she had encountered him since last night. A flutter of anxiety ran through

her. What would he have to say to her this morning?
Or she to him?

He looked down at her intently for a long uncomfortable moment before he remarked, perfectly
casually, 'You've started work already, I see.'

'Eh ... yes ... I'm just doing a few preliminary
sketches,' answered Louise, keeping her voice level
with effort.

His eyes held hers and it was impossible to divine
what he was thinking, only to know that in spite of
the antagonism between them, she felt disturbed by
him in a strange and unfamiliar way that had
nothing to do with hostility.

He did not linger but went on his way, leaving her
feeling as though she had been dishevelled by a particularly strong wind, and yet the day was as still as
it could be.

Louise found it difficult to concentrate after the
encounter and was glad when Philippa joined her.
They chattered easily about London, Philippa's
home in Hertfordshire, and her various jobs as a
teacher and governess.

'Selena and Simon go to school locally at present,'
she said, 'and I teach them when we're in England,
if it doesn't coincide with school holidays. Selena will
be going to boarding school in England soon, and I
suppose Simon will too eventually.'

'They're quite a handful,' said Louise.

Philippa laughed. 'Sometimes! But they're bright
and I love my job. Amber is a sweet person and not
as flighty as she sometimes appears. She's a wonderful
mother and never neglects her children. She's no
social butterfly, she wasn't even when Sir Peter was
alive.' Philippa sighed. 'He was a doll! So good-

looking, even in his sixties. Of course you know all
about him?'

'Not as much as I would like,' confessed Louise. 'I
wish I could have known him. It's going to be difficult painting him from photographs. What was he
really like, Philippa?'

Philippa considered for a moment or two. 'He was
. . . a good man, I suppose you'd say. He was charming, friendly, even flippant at times, but he had a
serious side, and his concern for people was real. He
put a total commitment into everything he did, from
establishing the veterans' home to car racing.' She
paused thoughtfully, pursing her lips. 'I don't know
how to put it . . . but I always felt I didn't know him
fully. He was . . . well, too good to be true. He's very
highly respected around here, of course, a kind of
saint.'

Louise remarked, 'Perhaps it's hard to believe in
people who seem faultless because we know we aren't
ourselves.'

Philippa nodded. 'I shouldn't have said that, I
suppose. It sounds churlish. After all, there's no
doubt that he was a hero and a philanthropist, and I
never heard of him doing a mean act. You know he
virtually saved the whole village from extermination
during the war?'

Louise shook her head. 'I didn't. I haven't read
his biography yet.'

'Well, the Germans were going to take reprisals
for attacks on their men, but he turned the tables on
them by capturing the Commandant and holding
him hostage. I don't know all the details, but they'll
be in the biography, I expect. There'll be quite a
celebration in the autumn—the book, your portrait,

and a memorial plaque. Les Deux Croix is really going to town on it.'

'It all makes me feel rather nervous about painting his portrait,' confessed Louise.

'If you want to talk to someone about Peter,' suggested Philippa, 'try Henri Leveque, although if your French isn't too good, that might be tedious. Best talk to Roland. He knew him as well as anyone.' She smiled meaningfully. 'Don't fall for him, though!'

'Roland? That's not very likely,' Louise retorted. She doubted too that Roland would be willing to help her, and she had little inclination to seek his help in the circumstances.

'You wouldn't be the first,' said Philippa candidly. 'I've been madly in love with him for years, but not a chance. Besides, any woman who looks like getting her claws into Roland is likely to have her eyes scratched out by Chantal!'

'Chantal d'Arbrisseau?'

'Who else? Wait until you meet her! She's away with her family in America at the moment, but they'll be back in a few weeks, and if you're still here, she'll be as suspicious as hell. She's eighteen, very beautiful, knows it, uses it, and is as jealous a little wildcat as you'll encounter. Keep well away from her, and never so much as look at Roland when she's around.' She laughed gaily. 'The trouble is she's only his second string, and that must be a bit galling, although she'll never admit defeat until he actually marries Amber.'

'I thought that was a foregone conclusion,' said Louise, remembering Céleste's remarks.

'Most people believe so,' affirmed Philippa. 'He lost her to Sir Peter in the first place, so they say,

which puzzled many people, including no doubt
Roland himself. After all, he was more her age, and
he's quite a dish, you must admit. All that quiet
brooding passion just waiting to be unleashed! It
makes your skin prickle just to think of it.'

Louise wondered what Philippa would say if she
told her about her encounter with Roland last night.
Needless to say she did not.

Philippa was racing on, 'Of course Sir Peter was
very distinguished and she was madly in love with
him. I don't think she ever looked at another man,
and to Roland she was just a sister. He's never shown,
not so you'd notice, that he's still in love with her,
but the gossips insist upon it. He's never married, for
one thing. Anyway, time will tell. It's my guess that
after the commemoration is over, something will
happen.' She sounded very sure.

'Do you think there's anything already agreed
between them?' asked Louise.

Philippa shrugged. 'I don't honestly know.
Amber's still confused and unhappy, but I believe
she's changing slowly, and once all the fuss over Sir
Peter is behind her she may feel free to fall in love
again. Roland is doubtless biding his time until it
happens. He wouldn't want to lose her a second time
by bad timing, would he?' She stood up. 'Well, I'd
better gather in the flock. It's nearly lunchtime. See
you presently, Louise.'

She walked off, leaving Louise to reflect idly on
their conversation, as she was to do from time to
time throughout the rest of the day.

That evening Amber brought out the photograph
albums and some press cuttings, and for the first time
Louise saw the man whose portrait she was to paint.

'Peter hated having photographs taken,' explained Amber. She laughed. 'He wouldn't have any of these cluttering up the mantelpiece in the drawing room either!' She looked concerned suddenly. 'Is it going to be too difficult, Louise?'

They were comfortably ensconced in the small sitting room, alone, since Roland had abruptly excused himself after dinner, and Philippa had gone to her room saying she had some letters to write.

Louise took a long deep breath. 'It will be difficult,' she admitted candidly. 'But not impossible, I hope.' She said this with more conviction than she felt.

'Well, take the albums,' said Amber, 'and all the other material so you can pore over it as and when you like. I'll give you the proofs of the book too.' She added, 'I think I've told you as much as I can about Peter. Roland might be helpful—if he's willing to co-operate. He's still rather angry with me at the moment.'

Louise did not answer. She just hoped that as the days passed, Roland would accept the situation and become co-operative.

The next morning Amber told Louise that she had made an appointment for them to see the Mayor the following afternoon. However, it seemed unlikely that it would be kept when Philippa came into the dining-room for lunch the next day and announced that Amber would not be down as she had one of her migraines. She had asked Philippa to cancel the appointment.

'I'd better do it straight away,' said Philippa, hovering in the doorway. 'Don't wait for me, please.'

'Just a minute . . .' Roland spoke suddenly just as

she was about to leave them again. She turned questioningly. He said, 'I'll take Louise.'

Philippa looked doubtful. 'But surely Amber will want . . .' she began.

Roland cut her short with a look. 'I'm sure Louise and I can handle the situation, and it's rather short notice to cancel the appointment. We don't want to upset Mayor Duval, do we?'

Philippa cast a look at Louise which said, 'It's not my place to argue.'

'I was intending to go that way myself this afternoon, to see the Rameaux,' said Roland with equanimity, 'so we can easily kill two birds with the one stone.'

Louise, however, felt it was just another example of his overbearing manner. She was not sure Amber would be too happy about it.

Philippa came back into the room and took her place at the table. 'Well, that's all right then,' she said, but sounded equally doubtful.

After lunch Louise ventured to go and see Amber, as she did not want to go with Roland unless Amber approved, and it was still not too late to cancel the arrangement if Amber insisted. Rather to her surprise, Amber enthusiastically supported the idea.

'Oh, good,' she said, in a small suffering voice. 'I didn't want to cancel the appointment when I'd only just made it, but I couldn't let you go alone. Don't let them browbeat you, Louise—no, Roland will see that they don't, I'm sure.' She smiled happily. 'I think this must mean he's forgiven me!'

Louise was not so sure, but she hoped Amber was right. Later that afternoon she found herself sitting beside Roland in his powerful big grey car, heading towards Les Deux Croix. There was an uncomfortable silence between them which was not broken until they reached the village square where Roland parked the car in the shadow of some mediaeval buildings.

'This is the Town Hall and offices,' he informed Louise, 'and we're on time.'

Louise glanced up at the clock tower, set in sombre grey stone. The clock began to strike four o'clock. Immediately her nervousness returned. She was anxious because she feared the mayor might be rather put out because Amber had chosen another artist to replace his preference, and a girl at that. Oh, why, she thought, do I always treat every new encounter as though it's a visit to the dentist!

She wished now that Amber had been able to come; she was not wholly confident that Roland would provide the kind of support she would need at this interview. She was apprehensive all the way up the massive staircase, and felt positively tongue-tied when she was ushered into the mayoral chamber and was faced with half a dozen men who eyed her with curiosity and not a little Gallic approval. Somehow, that made them a little less intimidating, and she immediately felt more at ease.

She was glad Roland had accompanied her, as her French was totally inadequate to the situation and the officials' English not entirely satisfactory. However, with Roland interpreting when necessary, and Louise injecting a few words of her careful school French into the discussion, the interview went tolerably well. Louise was soon aware that any initial antagonism towards her that there might have been was quickly melting away.

They showed her where the portrait was to be hung, beside the gold-lettered roll of honour, and alongside a plaque commemorating Sir Peter's exploits in the Resistance and his liberation of the village. She was handed a copy of the citation, and then the size of the painting was discussed at length. They would prefer something large, the mayor declared, running his eye doubtfully over Louise's slender frame as though querying whether she was physically capable of executing a large portrait. She took her courage in both hands and said she would do whatever they wanted. In turn they smilingly agreed to whatever fee she felt her work commanded, and not an eyelid was batted when she named the figure she had decided to ask.

At the end of the interview they all shook her hand vigorously, and paid her compliments, and Louise felt that it had not gone too badly. Even Roland condescended to say so as they were walking down the front steps of the Town Hall afterwards.

'You had them eating out of your hand, Louise. I believe they've gone away believing you actually speak French like a native! They didn't even notice me.' He laughed. 'That's Frenchmen for you! A pretty woman wins hands down every time. Why, they even reckon they've got a bargain, I'm sure!'

'I only hope I can deliver the goods,' Louise commented.

His eyebrows rose. 'You don't doubt you can do it, surely?'

'I'm a little worried. Sir Peter is very two-dimensional to me at the moment. I need to flesh him out a good deal more before I can even begin . . . if I'm to paint the real man, not just a copy a photograph.' She did not expect him to understand.

To her surprise he said, 'You mean being unable to use your own assessment of the man inhibits you?'

'Exactly . . . although I don't pretend to be an infallible judge of character.'

'Your pictures at the Profile Gallery showed remarkable perception,' he said, and Louise was astonished. She had imagined that he was there merely as an escort to Amber, and that his interest in her work had been only polite.

Now he was looking at her with that characteristically intent and enigmatic gaze, and it seemed he was turning over something in his mind. Louise waited for him to speak, but he did not. Instead, a voice suddenly called loudly across the square:

'Roland!'

They both turned, and Louise saw a tall, dark-haired girl running like a young gazelle towards them. Her eyes were shining, her dark hair flying, her cheeks flushed. As she came up to Roland, apparently oblivious of Louise, she stood on tiptoe and kissed him full on the mouth. 'Roland, *chéri* . . .' Her voice was low, husky, and the large dark eyes upturned to his face very possessive.

Louise noticed that his arms had folded around the girl and still clasped her loosely. He was speaking rapidly to her in French. It was clear that her appearance was unexpected and that he was dismayed by it.

Now she was speaking animatedly, and Louise, who had shrunk back, not wishing to intrude on a private matter, caught only a word here and there which revealed nothing of the trend of their conversation. Then Roland gestured with one hand in her direction, and they both turned to Louise. Roland started towards her and the girl tucked her arm pro-

prietorially through his, giving him another adoring
look.

For Louise the girl's look changed to one of
haughty disdain, as she looked her over critically.
Louise suddenly felt shabby and out of fashion, even
more so than she did with the exquisitely dressed
Amber. This girl had not only expensive clothes,
but a natural *chic* that only French girls seem able to
achieve. She wore her dark red suede suit, cream silk
blouse and soft leather boots with an air of casual
elegance that made Louise envious. Her own tweed
suit, she felt, looked very ordinary by contrast.

'May I present Louise Peterson,' said Roland.
'Louise, this is Mademoiselle Chantal d'Arbrisseau,
daughter of a neighbour of ours. 'I'm sure Amber
has mentioned General d'Arbrisseau.'

'*Enchantée, mademoiselle,*' murmured Chantal, with
no great sincerity.

Louise replied, 'How do you do?' and realised now
why Roland had seemed surprised to see the girl.
She was supposed to be holidaying in the States.

'It is such a surprise,' said Chantal, in attractively
accented English, 'to find that Amber is returned so
soon. We are all doing things no one expects. Roland
did not expect us to return yet, and here we are!' She
sighed exaggeratedly, and her eyes flicked from
Louise, with suspicion, back to Roland with adoration. 'It is Papa's fault. We were having a glorious
time and he receives this telegram saying they want
to hold his exhibition much earlier, so he insists we
come home . . .'

'They're bringing the exhibition date forward?'
Roland's voice was sharp.

Chantal pouted prettily. 'Yes. But it doesn't

matter. I will persuade Papa to go to Cannes for a few weeks soon, and you must come down sometimes, *chéri.*'

'I'm rather busy at the moment,' said Roland, with an evasiveness that suggested to Louise that he found Chantal's blatant adoration rather embarrassing.

'I do not believe that,' said Chantal, still pouting. 'I am sure you can be spared. Our vines manage to grow without Papa forever poking them in the ribs!'

'You are growing up irresponsible,' said Roland, rather dourly.

Chantal replied haughtily, 'I *am* grown up!' She shot a swift glance at Louise and her lips curled in a meaningful smile. 'As you very well know, Roland.'

He was looking at his watch. 'I'm sorry, Chantal, but we must go. I presume you don't need a lift?'

'No . . .' Again her eyes ran speculatively over Louise, and it was clear that she was mentally assessing whether she was any threat to her relationship with Roland. Louise was taken aback by the naked jealousy in the young girl's eyes, and decided she would not like to be a rival to her.

Chantal said sweetly, 'We must have a little party, Roland, as we are all back together. I will speak to Maman.' She gave an exaggerated sigh. 'Anything to break the monotony!' She added carelessly, 'How is Amber?'

'She has a migraine today,' Roland explained briefly.

'Oh, poor Amber. She is always having the migraine.' She made it sound, Louise thought, like something Amber did deliberately.

Roland opened the car door for her and she got

in. As she settled herself in her seat, she caught a glimpse of Chantal again openly embracing Roland, and she wondered if she behaved so blatantly when Amber was present.

Chantal waved a languid hand. '*Au revoir, mademoiselle*. I hope to see you again soon.' Louise knew she didn't really mean it.

Roland got in and they drove out of the square in silence. Louise suddenly could think of nothing to say. She was aware of Roland sitting rather tight-lipped and preoccupied beside her, and suspected he would not welcome small talk. He seemed in an even more sombre mood than before, the encounter with Chantal having chased away his rather more jovial mood after the successful interview at the Town Hall.

Louise, pondering on it, decided that he must have quite a problem handling the situation with his two women so that the outcome was to his advantage. And was there a third, as Amber suspected? Louise, glancing at his profile, thought it quite possible. She did not doubt that he was a passionate man, and while he still hoped to marry Amber, it was probably wise to keep Chantal at arm's length, since she appeared to be hot-blooded and impressionable and could cause him embarrassment if he became too involved with her. But, if he therefore had other affairs, surely they could be conducted without having the château empty for the purpose. His almost desperate lengths to achieve that still puzzled Louise.

They had driven out through the main entrance to the estate, but now they were returning by a different route, so that Roland could call on a family of estate workers. Louise remained in the car while

Roland went into the house. After a few minutes he came out, accompanied by a man and his wife, with whom he exchanged a few final pleasantries before getting back into the car. Judging by the effusive thanks bestowed on him by the couple, he had done them a considerable favour. Louise, although curious, since she had not thought of Roland as being a considerate man, did not dare to ask.

A few minutes later they were climbing a rather steep hill which brought them to a point behind the woods that flanked the château on two sides, and were almost at the top, when the car's engine suddenly gasped and spluttered and finally died.

'Damnation!' exclaimed Roland, pulling on the handbrake. He glanced at Louise. 'I think we've had it.'

'Had it?'

'This is exactly what happened to Amber, so she said. She got the road patrol, but the mechanic wasn't sure what was causing it. He got it going again for her, and they thought it must just have been dirt in the petrol.' He continued to press the starter, but nothing happened. He got out and impatiently peered into the engine, then came back and said, 'I can't see anything obvious.'

'We're not far from the château, are we?' said Louise. She had caught a glimpse of it beyond the woods as they were climbing the hill, but it was out of sight at the moment.

'No, not far,' answered Roland. He added decisively, 'It's probably a waste of time my tinkering with it. It's a garage job. It'll have to be thoroughly overhauled. We'll leave it here and walk. Do you mind?'

'Not at all. I enjoy walking,' said Louise promptly.

'It's getting dark anyway. You wouldn't be able to see to do anything for much longer.'

She got out. The sky was still tinged with gold although the sun had set some time ago. Louise stood for a moment looking at the scene. Roland came to her side. 'Almost like a painting, isn't it?'

'Yes! Just what I was thinking.' Louise looked up at him in surprise. 'It has the . . . texture of a painting. But what a struggle it would be to capture those colours. They change . . . mingle . . . tantalise. Nature is a better artist than any human will ever be.'

'Landscape is not your particular forte, though?'

'I like to paint landscapes sometimes. I hope to do a little while I'm here, if there's time.'

'You might find an eager buyer in the General,' remarked Roland, a trifle dryly. 'He's an avid art collector.' There was a note of derision in his voice.

'You mean Mademoiselle d'Arbrisseau's father?'

'General Raoul d'Arbrisseau,' he agreed. 'He's going to exhibit the pictures he bought from Peter in Paris very soon. It's quite an important small private collection and he's very proud of it.' There was something in his tone that Louise could not identify. He sounded antagonistic towards both the exhibition and the General. He was looking at her, again with an expression that suggested he was about to say something, then he looked away as though he had abruptly rejected it.

'Come on,' he said, 'or it'll be dark before we reach home. We have a fair distance to walk.'

Leaving the car at the side of the road, they continued on foot, with silence a palpable barrier between them again. After a few minutes, Roland said,

'We can turn off through the woods here. The road skirts right around them and will take much longer, but there's a short cut we can take.' He turned off down a well worn track into the trees and Louise reluctantly followed. She realised as she trailed a little behind him that she did not entirely trust Roland Winterhaven.

He turned a short distance farther on, when she was still lagging behind. 'What's the matter? Am I going too fast for you?'

'No.'

His smile mocked her. 'Are you afraid of me?'

'Yes!' she retorted. He could make her angry so easily.

He waited for her to catch up. 'Well, you needn't be. I apologise for my previous behaviour. It was a piece of play-acting that rebounded on me, and I suppose it served me right. I underestimated you, Louise. I won't play any more tricks on you, I promise. I have no evil designs on you. Now, come along . . .'

Louise remained where she was, staring at him. His apology had quite taken her breath away.

He reached for and clasped her hand as though she was a recalcitrant child, and instinctively she resisted him, but he refused to let go. Consequently she moved forward with a sudden jerky movement, caught her toe on some obstruction in the path and fell forward to be caught expertly in his arms.

Momentarily they both stiffened at the unexpected contact, and their eyes met and locked, not in a re-opening of hostilities, but something quite different, yet to Louise almost as frightening. Roland calmly bent his head and kissed her. It was not a kiss of passion or fury, not a kiss calculated to make her think him a brute and drive her away, but a kiss of such exquisite tenderness that Louise, in spite of herself, felt she was melting in his arms like icecream on a warm road. She found she had no resistance to this unexpectedly gentle caress, only an involuntary response to the tentative probing of his lips, while his arms held her not as a prisoner, but as lightly as though she was a delicate flower.

When he released her she could only look at him in astonishment.

'That was a bit out of character,' she whispered, emotionally shattered.

A smile began at the corners of his mouth and his face was no longer hard and arrogant, but soft, and there was a teasing glint in his eyes.

'Not really,' he murmured. 'I just wanted to prove I'm not always a man of such violent passions as you might have supposed.'

CHAPTER SIX

NEVER, Louise thought, as she changed for dinner, had she been so utterly confused by a man as by Roland Winterhaven. She thoroughly disliked him, utterly distrusted him, and yet this evening she had been completely disarmed by him. And that had been very unwise.

Could he possibly be the same man who had forced himself upon her with brutal passion, who had kissed her so tenderly in the woods this evening? And which was the real Roland Winterhaven?

She changed into a deep blue crêpe dress with a demure white Peter-Pan collar and cuffs, red buttons and a narrow red belt. She sighed as she looked at her reflection in the mirror. She would never have the elegance of Amber Winterhaven, or the *chic* of Chantal d'Arbrisseau. Strange that two such dissimilar women should attract Roland, she mused idly, and found herself hoping that he would marry Amber, not Chantal.

As she brushed her hair and applied her make-up, she was still thinking about the afternoon. She could not banish the memory of Roland Winterhaven's lips on hers and she wished she had not unconsciously responded. No doubt it gave him great satisfaction to find yet another woman attracted to him, especially one who had shown such previous antipathy.

'Just how many strings to your bow have you got?' Louise asked her own reflection as though she was speaking to him. 'I shall certainly not become one of them,' she determined aloud.

Glancing at her watch, she realised that she was dawdling and that it was almost time for dinner. She dusted a powder puff across her cheeks and nose, then hurried downstairs. She was almost at the foot of the stairs when Henri Leveque crossed the hall. He did not look up, apparently not having seen her. He seemed in rather a hurry.

'*Bonsoir*, Henri,' called Louise, but the man did not hear.

Louise heard a sharp chink as he crossed the hall, but it was not until she reached the bottom of the stairs that she realised he had dropped a bunch of keys.

'Henri!' she called, but he was already hurrying along a corridor away from her. Louise picked up the keys and dashed after him. It was gloomy in the corridor as the lights had not yet been turned on there, but she saw him just ahead of her, and was sure that he went into the library.

She followed, entering the room only a few seconds after him, but found to her surprise that he was not there, 'Henri?' she called, and then, switching on the light, walked right into the room. It was odd that he had not switched on the light himself. He did not appear, however, to be in the room at all.

'How odd,' murmured Louise. 'How very odd.' She tossed the keys to and fro in her hands. She must have been mistaken, she thought, and he had not come into the library after all. He must have gone into one of the rooms on either side. She checked, but everywhere was in darkness and there was no Henri. She decided not to waste any more time but to give the keys to Roland. When she entered the drawing room, Roland, Amber and Philippa were already there and wondering where she was. Amber had recovered from her migraine and though a little pale, was her usual lively self.

Roland met Louise's gaze with a steady look, but nothing in his expression betrayed the recent incident in the wood, or his extraordinary behaviour on her first night. He might have been a complete stranger she was meeting for the first time.

'Sherry?' he aked.

Louise nodded. 'Thank you.' She held out the keys. 'Henri dropped these a few moments ago in the hall. I called out and ran after him because I was sure he went into the library, but he wasn't there, or in any of the other rooms. Perhaps you would return them to him, Roland.'

The blandness left Roland's face and for a moment he looked both startled and relieved. He said, 'Thank you, Louise. Henri will be looking for them. I'd better find him straight away.'

Philippa laughed. 'If he hasn't been spirited away supernaturally. The château is supposed to be haunted, isn't it?'

'If it is, I've never seen a ghost.' Roland spoke rather sharply.

'Nor I,' said Amber lightly.

'I expect I shall find Henri having his dinner,' said Roland. 'So if you'll excuse me for a few minutes . . .' He poured a glass of sherry for Louise, handed it to her, and abruptly left them.

'Tell us all about your afternoon,' demanded Amber, as he went out. 'You were a great success, so Roland says.'

'I couldn't have done without his help,' said Louise, and proceeded to describe the meeting with the mayor and the decisions reached. Amber listened eagerly, nodding with satisfaction and murmuring her approval.

Louise was telling her how they had encountered Chantal d'Arbrisseau when Roland returned.

Amber turned to him. 'So Chantal and family are back. What a surprise! I thought they intended staying in America for another few weeks.'

'The General's exhibition has been brought forward,' explained Roland, in a rather clipped tone. To Louise he seemed worried, and preoccupied. 'Some rearrangement of the gallery's schedule was necessary.'

Amber said rather wryly, 'Our dear General is going to enjoy himself hugely playing the astute art collector with Peter's paintings.'

Roland, who was staring absently into his drink which he had just poured, did not comment. He seemed to have drifted right away from the conversation all at once.

Amber went on, 'I expect Chantal is furious. She loves the bright lights and thinks living in the country is being buried alive.' She cast a sidelong glance at Roland and winked at Louise and Philippa. 'The only thing that interests her here is Roland.'

The mention of his name jerked him to attention. Amber teased, 'Go on, Roland, you know Chantal's crazy about you. Ever since she was a little girl and you used to give her piggyback rides, she's been madly in love with you and jealous of any other woman who speaks to you.'

He fabricated a smile. 'I hadn't noticed!'

Amber chortled. 'Hark at him! If that isn't the

understatement of the year! I bet even Louise could see which way the wind blows, couldn't you, Louise?'

'She . . . was quite affectionate,' conceded Louise, stealing a glance at Roland, but his eyes met hers levelly, neither confirming nor denying.

Amber laughed, and a moment or two later Marie announced that dinner was ready.

That night Louise sat up in her room looking through press cuttings and snapshots of Sir Peter Winterhaven. She also began to read the proofs of the biography of him that was to be published later in the year. There was something that bothered her, some strange intuition that niggled in the back of her brain, but she could not quite put her finger on it. It was almost as though the handsome smiling face of the photographs was not being quite on the level with her.

When she finally laid the book down, only half read, it was after midnight. She switched out the light but did not close the shutters or curtains which she had opened earlier to admit the fresh, sweet-smelling night air. Moonlight streamed through the window, and after half an hour of lying wakeful, Louise knew she would never sleep unless she shut it out. She rose and went to the window, pausing by the open casement to look out across the moonlit countryside. The lake glittered and the woods crowded dark and forbidding beyond it. Suddenly she wanted to go for a walk. Without thinking twice, she obeyed the impulse. She slipped on a jacket over her thin nightdress, slid her feet into her sandals, and quietly tiptoed downstairs and out on to the terrace.

It was chilly but not freezing. The sky was clear

and starry, with the moon hanging over the distant hills like a Hallowe'en lantern. Louise walked the length of the terrace, trying to conjure up Sir Peter Winterhaven as a flesh and blood person, and failing, partly because despite her efforts he remained a two-dimensional photograph, and partly because her mind kept sidestepping into thoughts of Roland, and remembering the feel of his lips on hers.

She looked up at the night sky and tried to imagine parachutists descending, the criss-crossing of searchlights, the sound of anti-aircraft fire, tried to *feel* what it must have been like dropping behind enemy lines, working with the Resistance, always within a hair's breadth of death. Nothing in her experience could help her.

'I can't do it,' she whispered at last. 'I can't paint the portrait. I couldn't do him justice. Amber will have to find someone else.'

Depressed, she paused at the edge of the terrace, and turned to walk back in the opposite direction. Suddenly she jumped with fright as a hand touched her arm and Roland's voice said, 'Louise . . .' Looking up at him she saw that he was very displeased.

'I thought perhaps you were sleepwalking,' he said, his fingers digging into her arm.

'No.' Louise clutched her jacket around her, conscious suddenly of the flimsiness of her night attire, her tumbled hair and the lateness of the hour. Roland was still fully dressed, and she wondered vaguely what he was doing out so late. He, like everyone else, had said he was going to bed at eleven o'clock.

'Well, what the hell are you doing out here at this

time of night?' he rapped out angrily, not letting go of her arm, and shaking her impatiently.

His tone riled her. 'Is there anything wrong with taking a walk in the moonlight?' She jerked away from him.

'It seems rather odd,' he said suspiciously, 'snooping around after midnight.'

'Snooping? Why on earth should I snoop?' He seemed unreasonably angry with her, and this reversion to his former antagonism was in such sharp contrast to his softer treatment of her earlier, she could not help but feel that this afternoon's apology in the woods must have been a lapse he now regretted.

'I would be obliged if you would not indulge in nocturnal rambling,' he said crisply.

'Why?'

His face in the moonlight was grim, his eyes narrow, his mouth a tight line. 'You might be mistaken for a prowler.'

She smiled faintly. 'Oh, I see. You thought I was a burglar. Have you been bothered?'

'From time to time,' he answered testily, Louise felt sure he was making up excuses, but couldn't imagine why. He added, 'For your own safety, I would suggest you remain in your room at night.'

Louise answered archly, 'I thought I had nothing to fear from you now.'

'Do you always have to argue about everything?' he demanded in a surly tone.

'Only when people are being unreasonable,' Louise replied. 'I don't see why I shouldn't take a moonlight stroll if I feel like it, and I'm sure there's no danger, but since I'm a guest and you're the boss, I suppose I must defer to your wishes, irrational though they seem. As a matter of fact I feel quite sleepy now, so goodnight!'

She swept haughtily past him, walking quickly back towards the door she had come out of.

He called softly, 'Louise . . .'

She stopped, turned her head and said, 'Yes?'

Roland caught up with her. 'I'm sorry . . . I shouldn't have spoken to you like that. You only came out because you couldn't sleep?'

'Yes, why else would I?'

He shrugged, his eyes meeting hers searchingly.

She felt that some explanation was necessary. 'I'm having difficulty forming a clear picture of Sir Peter Winterhaven, and I felt rather restless. I'm not sure I'll be able to paint him after all.'

He seemed taken aback. 'But today you agreed . . .'

'And I told you I was worried about it. I still am. It's difficult to explain. There just seems to be something missing, that's all. Look . . . it doesn't matter, it's my problem and it will probably resolve itself.'

'You take your work very seriously, don't you?' His annoyance with her seemed to have dissipated in the past few minutes.

'Don't you?' she countered, disturbed more by the sudden change than his former anger.

She caught a glimmer of a smile. 'Of course! Does that make us two of a kind?'

'I have no idea.' Louise shivered suddenly. A breeze had sprung up and she had been out longer than she had intended.

'You're cold,' said Roland, 'you'd better go in.' His arm dropped lightly across her shoulders in a protective gesture, but instead of Louise feeling

soothed by his change of mood, she felt unaccount-
ably irritated.

She shook herself free again, said sharply,
'Goodnight, Roland,' and walked quickly towards
the door.

Back in her room she still could not sleep, but now
there was no pretence of tussling with her problem
over Sir Peter's portrait. Only one thought was uppermost in her mind. Roland Winterhaven was beginning to have an effect on her that she did not
welcome, and in future would use all her energies to
prevent.

As the days passed Louise's misgivings grew rather
than diminished and she wished that the interview
with the mayor had not taken place quite so soon, as
her acceptance of the commission to paint Sir Peter's
portrait was regarded as confirmed, and to decline
now would be letting them all down.

By the time the weekend came round again, she
felt totally restless and unable to concentrate even on
sketching the children, so since having a holiday was
part of her agreement, she decided to take the day
off and go sightseeing.

'I think I'll go to Amboise,' she told Amber, 'if
you don't mind?'

'Of course not! You do exactly as you please. I
said you were to regard this as a holiday and I meant
it.'

'Would the children like to come?' Louise asked,
thinking it might make a welcome break for Philippa
as well as Amber. It would also afford her an opportunity of observing them and their reactions in a
new situation.

Amber laughed. 'You're game! I'm sure they'd

love to go. They've never been to Le Clos-Lucé and
Simon would be fascinated by the models. I've
always been meaning to take him as soon as he was
old enough to appreciate them. But, Louise dear, do
you really want to be lumbered?'

'I'd love it,' Louise assured her sincerely.

There was no hesitation on the part of Selena,
Simon and Angela. They were delighted with the
projected expedition and were down waiting by her
car for Louise long before she was ready. When she
appeared, Roland was standing talking and laughing
with the children. They seemed very fond of their
Uncle Roland, Louise mused absently, and he was
always very tolerant with them, she had noticed.

He smiled at Louise, but his look held a little
reserve as though he was uncertain what her attitude
towards him was. She had seen little of him during
recent days and always she had felt this same reserve
in his manner towards her.

He said, 'Are you really taking these horrors out
for the day?'

'Uncle Roland, we are not horrors!' objected
Angela, with four-year-old dignity.

He rumpled her curls and she wriggled away from
him, giggling.

'We'll see what Louise has to say about that when
she returns,' he said.

'Why don't you come too, Uncle Roland,' said
Selena. 'You'd be company for Louise.'

Louise blushed as she found her eyes meeting
Roland's, which now twinkled with amusement. He
said lightly, 'I think Louise has enough to contend
with, taking you three. She won't want me around
as well.'

'Go on, come, Uncle Roland,' put in Simon, not

to be outdone. 'I don't want to be the only man!'

Roland laughed and shook his head. 'I'm much too busy . . .' He shot Louise a challenging look. 'Unless Louise wants to twist my arm.'

Louise was annoyed. She knew Roland was mocking her. He didn't want to come, was certain she didn't want him to, but he wanted to put her on the spot.

She shrugged indifferently. 'It's entirely up to you, Roland. I'm sure I don't mind, but if you're busy . . .'

To her surprise he said at once, 'Oh, well, I suppose I'm not all that busy. I could come if everyone wants me to.'

'Yes, Uncle Roland, come!' chorused the children.

'Just give me five minutes, then, to tell Henri.' He walked off rapidly, and Louise drew a deep breath. He was so unpredictable. She had an uneasy feeling that what had promised to be a carefree outing might be turning into an ordeal.

Within five minutes Roland had returned. Louise and the children were waiting in the car. He approached the driver's side.

'I'll drive if you like, Louise. I know my way around better than you do.'

Since this was true, Louise could hardly argue, although she felt sure his real reason for wanting to drive was because he didn't want to be seen being driven by a woman. She shifted across the seat and he slid behind the wheel.

Conversation between them was neither necessary nor possible as the children kept up a constant stream of chatter from the back, demanding either Louise's or Roland's attention continuously. Once Roland glanced at Louise with a wry smile.

'A taste of things to come?'

'What?'

He chuckled. 'You have the makings of an excellent parent, Louise. You know instinctively how to handle children—and I don't mean just painting them.'

'You seem to handle these three pretty well yourself.'

'They practically are mine,' he observed, with a laugh. 'I've known them since they were born.'

And of course soon they would be legally his, Louise thought, if he married Amber. There would be no problems there—the children obviously adored him.

After a silence he asked, 'Have you been to any of the big châteaux hereabouts?'

Louise shook her head. 'Not inside. I was here a few years ago with a group from art school, but we didn't have much time.'

'How would you like to visit one of them before lunch? Do you remember Chenonceaux?'

'I do!' Louise said, enthusiastically. 'I thought it was one of the most beautiful places I'd ever seen. We painted it.'

'Then we'll go there today.'

This, Louise thought, must be Roland at his most amiable. It was hard to reconcile this smiling man with the violent brute of her first night at the château, even with the totally different man who had so tenderly kissed her in the woods the day the car broke down. Today he was someone else again, the charming, affable uncle, and Louise suddenly felt more relaxed with him than she had so far. Her earlier unease vanished and she began to enjoy herself.

They toured the château and the children were very well behaved and did not once complain they were bored. Even little Angela seemed to enjoy looking at the lavish furnishings, the tapestries and paintings.

Roland said musingly, 'I wonder what they were really like.'

'Who?' Louise dragged her attention from a painting to answer him.

'The elegant ladies who once graced these castles. Diane de Poitiers for instance, Catherine de Médici, Louise de Lorraine . . .' He paused on the last name, smiling at her. 'I wonder what that Louise was like—small and pretty with intelligent eyes, perhaps—like you!'

'What have I done to deserve such flattery?' Louise asked, amused as well as taken aback by the flirtatious tone of his comment.

He laughed softly, and looked down at her with a strange expression. 'You fascinate me.'

'Don't most women?' Louise countered.

'Some more than others.'

'I think we'd better gather the children,' said Louise quickly, half because she had just realised they had strayed and half because she wanted to get away from his searching gaze. Roland Winterhaven was not behaving at all like himself today, and she was disconcerted.

As it was a fine sunny day, Roland suggested they have a picnic lunch. In Amboise they went into a pâtisserie and to their great delight the children were allowed to choose exactly what they wanted. Roland bought some cans of soft drink for them, and pochettes of white wine for himself and Louise.

'We'll have to manage without glasses,' he said, 'but this sunshine is too good to waste by sitting indoors for a meal.'

Louise agreed, and so, bearing their paper bags of goodies, they climbed up to a high place overlooking the grey-roofed town and the château. Roland spread a rug which Louise had kept in the car, fortunately, on the ground and they hungrily set about having lunch.

Presently the children drifted a little way off to play and Roland stretched out, his large frame reaching beyond the end of the rug. He clasped his hands behind his head, and sighed with contentment. Louise had not seen him so composed before.

'Ah, this is the life ... food, wine and a pretty woman!' He looked sidelong at her in a teasing way.

Louise stretched out too, on the far side of the rug. 'Am I supposed to agree?'

He frowned. 'You're still edgy with me, Louise. Am I not yet forgiven for the appalling way I treated you? Don't you trust me still?'

'Of course I've forgiven you,' she said, and thought, 'But I'm wary of you. You affect me in a way I know is dangerous.'

Suddenly he rolled over towards her, and lay with his face very close to hers, his eyes, shadowed by the thick lashes, inscrutable. His mouth quivered slightly as he hesitated for a moment before pressing his lips to hers. The sun was warm, the children's shouts were close by, but they were far enough away and too absorbed in what they were doing to notice. Louise discovered to her dismay that where Roland was concerned, her will was suddenly weak. She let him kiss her, and hardly realising she was doing it, she lifted her hand and ran her fingers around his neck and into his hair. It was only when his hand slid caressingly across her breasts and she felt the warmth of his fingers through her blouse that she pushed him away.

'Roland . . . no, don't . . .'

'Why not?' he asked lazily. 'I like it, so do you . . .'

Louise was angry. He was going to marry Amber, or if not her, Chantal. For her there could only be flirtation, and she didn't want that, not with anyone, and least of all with Roland Winterhaven. With him she would only want . . . `She snapped off the treacherous thought resolutely. Such a thing was crazy, impossible.

'I don't want to be just one of your casual affairs,' she said. She started to get up, but he pulled her down on to the rug.

'Louise, you wouldn't be . . .' His touch was gentle, but there was a passionate fire in his eyes. She knew she must not believe him.

'Where are the children?' she cried, and managed to scramble out of his grasp, and to her feet. 'Selena!' she called. 'Simon! Angela! Come along!'

She felt hot and flustered, and a little lightheaded from the wine and Roland's attempt at lovemaking. Oh, why had she let him do it? Why had she responded? She had betrayed herself yet again in his arms and he was no doubt laughing at her for a gullible fool.

The children were not far away and came running obediently. Angela handed Louise a small posy of wildflowers, dandelions, daisies and a few shivering grass heads.

Louise smiled and thanked her as she made an

effort to pull herself together and act normally, but her thoughts were to remain in turmoil for the rest of the afternoon.

She walked through the castle of Amboise, and then the manor house of Le Clos-Lucé in a kind of daze, only half seeing everything. At Le Clos-Lucé she should have been as fascinated as Simon was with the models made from the drawings of Leonardo da Vinci, the collection of extraordinary machines designed by a man centuries before his time, but all she could think of was that moment on the hilltop, while the children played and the river flowed below, and briefly there had been only her and Roland in the world. She was on a path to deep hurt, she realised, unless she backtracked immediately.

They wandered through the grounds of the château and then walked back down to the town to where they had left the car, passing picturesque houses intriguingly built right into the rocky hillside. Roland repeated for her what the guide at Le Clos-Lucé had been telling them in French, but which Louise had not fully understood. She scarcely took it in even now, in English.

She was glad when they arrived back at the Château des Ormeaux. The children immediately rushed off to find Amber and Philippa, to relate their doings of the day. Louise went straight up to her room, glad of a respite in which to sort out her disordered feelings.

A few days later Louise started preliminary sketches of Sir Peter Winterhaven. She began tentatively, in the tower room studio, and at first she felt confident. After a while, however, her confidence ebbed and she kept screwing up her efforts and hurling them across the room in disgust. She was drawing lines, that was all, meaningless lines. A likeness perhaps, but anyone can draw a likeness, she told herself scornfully. A portrait must capture the essence of the man. Finally she abandoned her work and went for a walk. Outside it was warm and sunny with a light breeze, perfect spring weather, as it had been almost every day since she had come to France.

She strolled aimlessly for some time, finally ending up near the winery and the cellars which so far she had not visited. The cluster of buildings was some distance from the house, and she came upon it unexpectedly from a meandering path she had chosen to follow. The buildings looked deserted. There were workers out in the vineyards, she could see the occasional white hats or coloured scarves bobbing between the rows, busy at some task or other. But there were no grapes yet, and there would be none until late summer when the presses would begin to crush the juice from them to make the wine. She would be long since gone by then, she reflected, and felt for the first time a pang of regret. It was so beautiful here, and despite her problems, Roland and the portrait of Sir Peter, she was enjoying herself.

In an open shed, she found some fascinating examples of old wine-making machinery. She loitered for some time studying them, wishing someone was there to explain what everything was for, but there was no one about, it seemed.

Presently, out of increased curiosity, she ventured into the main building, which was rather gloomy and obviously not in use at present. As her eyes became accustomed she could see the outlines of machinery, huge vats and barrels, and so she walked in to investigate. She was wandering down a narrow passageway between stacks of barrels when from behind she felt a hand closing tightly around her forearm. She let out a stifled scream, and looked around into the steely grey eyes of Roland Winterhaven. He was not smiling and his amiable manner of a few days previously was today conspicuous by its absence.

'Roland, you gave me such a fright!' she exclaimed breathlessly.

'What are you doing down here?' The question was roughly spoken.

'I was . . . just looking around . . .' His tone made her feel guilty, as though she had trespassed.

He observed her coldly. 'Why didn't you ask me to show you around?'

'I . . . I didn't think of it. I was just wandering around and I happened to end up here.'

'If you want to see something, ask me first and I'll show it to you,' he said briskly.

Louise had the oddest feeling that he was not just angry with her, but apprehensive too, almost as though he had something to hide. She remembered his annoyance with her when she had gone for a walk in the moonlight. He had looked at her like that then too. But what could he have to hide? The idea seemed quite ridiculous.

'I didn't think I could do any harm just looking around,' she said. She added sarcastically because his manner irritated her, 'If you've got some secret wine-making process you're afraid I'll steal, you needn't worry. I wouldn't know it if I fell over it.'

His eyes had narrowed and he regarded her with

deep suspicion. Then all at once he seemed to relax. 'Well, now that you're here,' he said in a milder tone, 'I might as well show you everything and explain it to you.' A slight pause then as he looked over her shoulder at something. Louise turned and saw Henri Leveque, who seemed to have materialised from nowhere. He was very dusty as though he had been crawling about under the barrels. 'Ah, Henri,' said Roland loudly, then spoke to him in French, too rapidly for Louise to follow any of it. Her impression was, however, that Henri was reassuring Roland about something.

Henri acknowledged her greeting briefly, then shuffled away. With a complete change of manner, Roland now guided Louise around the winery, taking no end of trouble to explain to her the various stages of wine-making. When she mentioned the old machinery she had seen he immediately went outside with her and explained its uses. Louise found the tour immensely interesting and despite his disturbing proximity she managed to ask intelligent questions and to absorb most of what he was telling her.

Finally he said, 'Well, that's about all I can show you. Satisfied now?'

'Thank you. It was most interesting.'

He walked back to the house with her as it was lunch time, and they went upstairs together.

Outside her room, Louise paused and said, 'Thanks again for the tour, Roland.'

'Not at all, it was a pleasure,' said Roland, and dropped his hand on her shoulder. His eyes held hers with a lingering mixture of suspicion and speculation, almost as though once again he was about to say something more, but had changed his mind.

Instead his fingers slid across her bare neck and briefly strayed into her hair, making the nape of her neck tingle and her face flush pink. Her confusion seemed to amuse him greatly.

'See you at lunch,' she muttered hastily, and quickly escaped into her room.

CHAPTER SEVEN

THE days slid one into the other with astonishing ease so that Louise, always busy either with her sketching and painting, or taking short trips out sightseeing when she felt unable to work, was hardly aware of time passing. Roland she carefully avoided as much as possible, and he did not accompany her on a drive again. They met at meal times and that was about all.

A few days after the outing to Amboise, General d'Arbrisseau, his wife, Eloise, and Chantal came to the Château des Ormeaux for dinner. Louise felt rather nervous that evening as she dressed, as she always did when obliged to meet strangers, but particularly so tonight because she knew Amber was anxious to show them the painting Louise had half finished of the children as a group. Although Louise was pleased that Amber was delighted with it, she was nevertheless selfconscious of the fact that she was an unknown and very open to criticism. She did not believe that the General was as ignorant of art as Amber and Roland pretended.

She decided to wear her red dress because its colour always gave her confidence. She had not worn it since her first evening and so was slightly dismayed at first to find when she zipped it up that she had filled out quite a bit in the short time she had been at the château. She had been rather too thin before and her clothes had tended to hang on her a little. Now she surveyed herself anxiously in the mirror, but had

to admit that the closer fit was certainly more flattering, although she wondered if the neckline, which
now clung to and uplifted her more fully rounded
breasts, was not too revealing. She shrugged. There
was no need to be too modest!

When she went into the drawing room, expecting
the others all to be there, although she had not heard
the guests arriving, she found only Roland. He was
standing near the fireplace in which only a token fire
burned as the weather had turned quite warm. The
door was open when she walked in, but he appeared
not to notice her entering. She paused, observing
him for a moment as she tried to smooth the conflict-
ing feelings he always aroused in her. He seemed
rather dispirited. His shoulders were slumped and he
looked like a man with weighty problems.

As Louise crossed the room towards him, he looked
up. For a moment he still seemed to be far away in
his thoughts, and his expression underlined what his
whole demeanour suggested, that he was deeply
worried about something.

'Good evening, Louise,' he said at last. 'Sherry?'

'Thank you.' She accepted the glass from him and,
meeting those cool dark grey eyes under their lush
lashes, she experienced a new feeling—a strong desire
to help him, to ease whatever was troubling him.

She heard herself saying, 'Is anything wrong?'

He looked startled. 'Wrong? Why do you ask?'

Louise felt embarrassed. 'You looked rather morose
when I came in, as though you had something on
your mind.'

'I always have something on my mind,' he
answered, turning his glass slowly in his long square-
tipped fingers. 'Running an estate is a full-time
occupation full of problems.'

'Yes, I'm sure it is,' answered Louise, feeling she had presumed.

'But usually it's not hard to find solutions to those problems.' he went on.

Louise said boldly. 'I suppose it would be presumptuous of me to ask if I could help ... I mean, just talking about things sometimes helps.'

He gazed into the fire, then looked up and smiled at her, rather ironically, she thought. 'The time when you could have helped is long past,' he said, and there was a hint of bitterness in his voice.

Louise felt rebuked. 'What do you mean?'

He took her glass and placed it and his own on the table near them. Facing her, he took both her hands in his and said softly, 'Never mind.' His gaze swept over her and she saw that he was making a conscious effort to throw off his mood. 'How beautiful you are tonight! I like you in red.' His hands slid slowly and caressingly up her arms to her shoulders. Then one hand tilted her chin as he looked deeply into her eyes. 'You know, Louise, I could ...' His lips moved sensuously to make the words and drew closer to hers. Louise wanted to break away, to resist him, but could not. He seemed to have an irresistible power over her and his mouth drew hers like a magnet. She closed her eyes.

'Guests have arrived!' Philippa's strident tones shattered the spell.

Colour surged through Louise's cheeks as she turned and saw Philippa in the doorway. The governess's expression stated plainly that she had not missed the intimacy of the moment she had interrupted.

Roland, ever urbane, replied, 'Thank you, Philippa.' He turned to Louise. 'If you'll excuse me,

Louise, I'll go and greet them.'

Louise remained alone in the drawing room, sipping her sherry and waiting. She heard voices and laughter in the hall, and a few minutes later Roland came back accompanied by Raoul d'Arbrisseau, his wife and daughter.

The General was a bit of a bear, Louise decided, and his wife, a few years younger, was tall and haughtily glamorous. Chantal, who closely resembled her mother, treated Louise to a long critical appraisal before drawing Roland aside. She began to speak to him volubly in French, thus effectively snubbing Louise. A little bewildered by the mixture of French and English flying about, Louise was relieved when Amber finally appeared with Philippa.

Amber laughingly apologised as she greeted her guests. 'I'm so sorry, but I had trouble with a zip! It got stuck and neither Marie nor Céleste was able to unstick it. Philippa saved the day. I was beginning to feel I might be trapped in my dress for ever, neither quite in or quite out!'

Everyone laughed sympathetically and light-hearted conversation continued to flow. Louise was surprised to find herself the centre of attention for some time, but she was also well aware that Chantal regarded her with disdain. The French girl looked very sophisticated in a clinging cream silk dress that Louise knew must have come from one of the exclusive fashion houses. It swirled with tiny knife pleats, and its closely fitting bodice emphasised her softly rounded figure. The plunging back showed off the creamy smoothness of her neck and shoulders. She had pinned her hair up, letting tendrils escape at the temple, and the effect was to emphasise her high cheekbones and slightly slanted eyes. She was a very striking girl, Louise thought, and saw that Roland agreed, judging by the way he looked at her. But there was a hardness about her mouth that spoiled her beauty.

Once Louise caught a glance from Philippa, and the girl smirked meaningfully. Presently, as they were going to dinner, she whispered in Louise's ear, 'He's only playing around, Louise. Be careful!'

Louise tightened her lips. 'I know!' Well, she did, didn't she? She was well aware that advances from Roland were not to be taken seriously. He had probably trifled with Philippa, in the same way.

At dinner Louise was seated next to the General. Their conversation naturally gravitated to art.

'So you are to paint the portrait of Sir Peter Winterhaven,' he remarked, in excellent English.

'I haven't got very far with it yet.' Louise confessed.

'Difficult, difficult,' sympathised the General, 'with only photographs to guide you. Still, it is a good thing they are to commemorate him at last.'

Roland was sitting opposite Louise, and in spite of herself she found her eyes locked with his more often than she found comfortable. He still seemed a little preoccupied and she wished she knew what was worrying him so much. Why she should suddenly feel such concern for him, she did not know.

'If you would like to see the paintings,' the General was saying, 'you must do so before they go to Paris to be exhibited.'

Louise drifted back to him. 'Thank you . . . I would like to see them.'

Roland, who had not appeared to be listening,

said, 'I believe the exhibition date has been brought forward, General.'

'Yes. That's why we came home. I had not made arrangements about the insurance, and naturally I cannot allow the collection out of my house until they are adequately covered. I'm not happy with the firm I retained, so I am looking for someone expert to make an independent assessment.'

Amber, overhearing, put in, 'What about Edgar Benson? He valued them for Peter, General. Actually, he even sold two of them to Peter, if I remember rightly. He would certainly be the best person for you, wouldn't you agree, Louise?'

'Edgar is a recognised expert in Impressionist and post-Impressionist art,' agreed Louise.

Amber added enthusiastically. 'Why don't we ask him to come down and stay for a few days?' She smiled at Louise. 'I suspect you're missing him, Louise.' She glanced around the table and said teasingly. 'He's written to her twice already!'

'Amber, you have been prying!' exclaimed Chantal. 'Shame on you!' She looked imperiously at Louise. 'Is he your fiancé?'

Louise was embarrassed. 'No . . . we're just good friends. He's helped me a great deal.' She caught a look from Roland that was definitely reproachful.

Amber went on, 'We mustn't tease. One's love life should be private. But how about it, General, shall we ask Edgar to come?'

Madame d'Arbrisseau put in, 'I think that would be an excellent idea, Raoul.' She went on, 'Chantal was saying we ought to have a party, and I agree. It would be nice to have it while all the pictures are still with us. There will be so many gaps!'

'Oh, yes, Maman,' enthused Chantal. 'It will help

to relieve the boredom. Then, perhaps, when all this is settled we can go to Cannes for a few weeks. Do say yes, Papa!'

The General chuckled. 'It seems my decisions are now made for me by the women in the family. Very well, ask Monsieur Benson to come, and have your party. We will talk about Cannes later.'

'Why don't you telephone Edgar straight after dinner?' suggested Amber in her usual impetuous manner. 'He might be at home.'

Louise allowed them to persuade her. As she went to telephone she suddenly felt a great need to see Edgar, not for the romantic reasons the rest of the gathering supposed, but because she wanted him to look at her work, and criticise. Edgar was the only person whose judgment she could trust.

Edgar was delighted to oblige the General. 'Any excuse to see you, my love,' he said lightly. 'I can come down this weekend if that's convenient for everyone. Cathy can hold the fort. I had it in mind to go to Paris soon in any case, so I can see the people I want to see there and then drive on down to Château des Ormeaux at the weekend.'

'I'll just check with Amber,' said Louise. 'Hold on.'

Amber was agreeable and so was the General, so Louise ran back to the phone and confirmed it. The only person who showed no enthusiasm for the arrangements was Roland. Although he did not actually say so, his lack of enthusiasm and his slightly irritated look made Louise sure he disapproved. She could not imagine why, except that Roland did seem to disapprove in principle of anything that was not his idea. He was, Louise thought, stealing a glance at him later, while they were having coffee, a very enigmatic man.

As Edgar was now coming, Louise deferred making
a visit to the d'Arbrisseaux to see the pictures until
his arrival. Madame d'Arbrisseau had invited them
all to a party on the Saturday night he would be
there. According to Amber it was likely to be a fairly
lavish affair.

'Chantal will twist her father's arm,' said Amber
with a sly chuckle. 'She and her mother could
squeeze blood out of a stone!' Suddenly she exclaimed
with fervour, 'I am so tired of all my old dresses!
Let's go to Paris and buy something new!'

Louise was taken aback. Privately she had been
wondering which of her own rather ordinary dresses
would be remotely suitable for the fashionable gathering at the d'Arbrisseaux, but she had not considered buying a new one. Besides, she could not
really afford the kind of salon she was sure Amber
would patronise.

Amber read her thoughts and brushed them aside.
'I insist on giving you a present,' she said. 'And
Philippa, too. We will all three go to Paris and have
a spending spree.' Her eyes lit up at the prospect,
and although Louise had some misgivings she knew
it would be pointless arguing with her. Amber, with
her mind made up about something, was formidable,
as she had already discovered.

To Louise's surprise, when the impending expedition was announced, Roland raised no objections,
and even the prospect of Amber spending a considerable amount of money did not seem to aggravate
him. He even offered to drive them.

'I have some business in Paris,' he said, 'so we
might as well go together.'

Even Amber seemed astonished at his offer. She

impulsively went up to him and kissed him. 'Dear Roland,' she said, patting his cheek affectionately, 'how sweet of you!' His expression remained bland, and Louise wondered, not for the first time, if there was any commitment between them yet. If there was they would naturally want to keep it well hidden until after the commemoration of Sir Peter was over.

They left very early in the morning for the long drive to Paris, and once arrived, Roland dropped them off at their first destination, Amber's favourite fashion salon which, she had explained, was not one of the more renowned or expensive places, but a small exclusive place where you could buy quality ready-made gowns at sensible prices. Louise had smiled to herself. She had a feeling that Amber's idea of a sensible price might be rather different to hers.

But Philippa had urged earlier when learning of Amber's plan, 'Let her do it, Louise. She'll get a hell of a kick out of it. Splashing her money around is about the only pleasure she gets these days.'

'Lunch at Angélique's?' Roland enquired as they were getting out of the car.

'Are you going to be gallant and treat us?' asked Amber, with a sweet smile.

'Have I any alternative?' he replied, a twinkle in his eyes. 'Taking three glamorous ladies to lunch I shall be the envy of every Frenchman in the place!'

How mercurial he was, thought Louise, as they entered the salon, which displayed only a piece of pale rose silk and a cluster of feathers in the front window. One moment he was sombre and pre-occupied, the next teasing or gentle.

Her thoughts of Roland were soon supplanted, however, by the procedure of selecting gowns.

Madame Foulard, the proprietress of the salon, greeted them effusively. She was a tall, elegant woman with white hair dressed in Edwardian style. She called to two assistants and soon there was an array of dresses for Amber, Louise and Philippa to try on.

Slightly awed, Philippa whispered, 'I've never been in one of these places before. Bit scary, isn't it?'

Louise was reverently fingering one of the gowns. 'Feel the material . . . it's beautiful . . . so soft!'

Time flew as they tried on and paraded in the various dresses. Eventually Amber said to Louise. 'That's you, Louise! Don't you agree, Philippa?'

Louise twirled in the peacock blue silk dress with a flowing skirt and cinched waist, a deep neckline that was perhaps a little daring, but with soft folds that were caught together on the shoulders with diamenté clips. It fitted her perfectly and she rather fancied it herself. She was glad Amber approved. Philippa agreed, so Louise said she would have it. There was no price tag on it naturally, so Louise had no idea of its cost. She did not dare to ask.

Philippa then decided on a slinky silver gown, and Amber finally made up her mind to have a glamorous white and gold creation. Its Grecian style suited her graceful stature and classic style of beauty.

There were minor alterations to be made to both Amber's and Philippa's gowns, but Madame Foulard promised they would be done immediately and ready for them to collect on the way home. Well pleased with their purchases, they said their good-byes to Madame and her assistants and left the salon.

'Now, shoes,' said Amber, her eyes dancing with enthusiasm.

'It's almost lunchtime,' Philippa reminded her

anxiously. 'Roland will be waiting.'

Amber grinned. 'He'll wait! It won't take us long to buy some shoes. Louise must have the right colour to match her dress.'

Louise had not thought of shoes, and now she felt guilty for choosing a dress which would require new ones. Amber, however, would not listen to protests, and surged ahead to what she insisted was the 'best *magasin de chaussures* in Paris'. It certainly seemed so because there Louise did find shoes of exactly the right shade—at least she hoped it was.

'I'm sure it is,' said Amber, considering her choice, 'but if not we can come back when we have matched them to the dress.' That this would entail unwrapping a carefully done up parcel did not bother her in the least, and Louise forbore to mention it, knowing the difficulty would be brushed aside.

As Amber and Philippa also both bought new shoes, they were very late arriving at the restaurant for lunch. Louise half expected Roland to be angry, but he still seemed to be in an amiable mood. Indulgently he enquired if their shopping expedition had been successful, and when Amber teased him by saying they had been dreadfully extravagant, he did not even frown, but smiled resignedly. Perhaps, Louise thought, he had accepted that it was pointless trying to inflict his will on Amber, at least until they were married.

It was dark when they arrived back at the château. Amber had insisted on buying some cosmetics after lunch, and a few other things she needed as well, so by the time they collected their purchases from Madame Foulard and made sure that Louise's shoes were a good match, it was very late indeed.

'I don't know about you two,' said Amber, when

they arrived home, 'but I'm exhausted. But it was a successful day, wasn't it?'

'Perfectly,' agreed Louise.

'Fantastic,' said Philippa, and yawned.

Louise glanced at Roland who was helping to carry their parcels inside. Perhaps it had not been so perfect for him, but he had been remarkably patient throughout. She felt they ought to thank him, so she said:

'I think Roland deserves some applause for coping with three wayward females so uncomplainingly.'

Amber laughed, and she and Philippa clapped enthusiastically.

'Yes, thank you very much, Roland,' said Amber. She skipped across to him and kissed him.

Roland smiled at the other two, saying, 'Well, aren't you two going to reward me too!'

Louise was struck with sudden embarrassment, but Philippa boldly followed Amber's example and lightly pecked his cheek. Louise could hardly not do likewise so she too reached up to lightly brush his cheek with her lips. He turned his head slightly and instead her lips touched his briefly, and in so doing she caught a look from him that made her think of that day in Amboise, and the other times . . .

For the next couple of days Louise worked hard, spurred on by a sudden spurt of energy. She was outside on the terrace, starting a new version of the children in a group when Edgar arrived. He was earlier than she had expected and her heart gave a lurch of pleasure when she saw his car turn around in front of the château. She put down her palette and brushes and ran to greet him. He swung her into his arms and kissed her soundly, then held her away from him approvingly.

'You're looking wonderful,' he enthused. 'Pretty as a picture. How's it going?'

'Very well,' said Louise, cheered by the sight of him. 'The children have been very good and Amber is lovely. I couldn't have had a better commission.' She paused and kissed his cheek. 'Thank you, Edgar, for arranging it. I shall always be grateful.' There would be time enough later, she decided, to tell him about her problem with Sir Peter's portrait.

'Rubbish ... all in the line of business.' He brushed her gratitude aside as he always did and with his arm slung affectionately around her shoulders said, 'Come on, show me ...'

The children now crowded round excitedly, so that for a moment or two Louise was unaware that there was an observer of the scene. Roland was standing a little apart from them. He came forward to greet Edgar, a shade coolly, Louise thought, in some surprise.

The two men shook hands and they went into the house leaving Louise to pack up her painting gear, as she had decided it would be impossible to do any more today. Edgar came up to her studio presently and to her relief he was enthusiastic about her efforts so far.

'Yes ... yes ... you're doing very nicely,' he said, and Louise felt gratified. Perhaps his encouragement was all she needed to make Sir Peter come alive. She told him how she felt about it.

He listened and stroked his chin thoughtfully. 'I know what you mean. He's too much of a saint, that's the trouble, isn't it?'

Louise nodded. 'I think so. And yet in some of the photographs of him there's a hint of something I can't quite put my finger on . . . a weakness perhaps . . .'

'We all have them,' smiled Edgar. 'He was probably a jealous man.'

'I don't know that, that's the trouble,' said Louise. She spread her hands despairingly. 'Perhaps I'm just making excuses because I'm not capable . . .'

He gave her an impatient shake. 'Of course you're capable. Stop worrying about it. It'll come. You've got plenty of time.'

'I can't stay here much longer, though. I feel I'm imposing, despite what Amber says.'

'Amber told me she loves having you, that just your being here has cheered her up no end. She's rather lonely, Louise.'

'I know. She suffers a lot under that bright, lively exterior. It will be a relief when she can marry Roland, I suppose.'

Edgar looked mildly surprised. 'That's the way it is?'

'Well, everyone seems to think so, and that it wouldn't be tactful of them to say anything definite until after the commemoration for Sir Peter.'

'Hmm,' said Edgar. He went on, 'I gather we're all invited to a party tomorrow night at the d'Arbrisseaux'.'

'Yes. I'm feeling rather guilty because Amber insisted on buying me a new dress for it. She bought Philippa one, too. We all went up to Paris for the day. She's so generous!'

Louise was still feeling a little guilty about the dress the following evening when she lifted the soft silky folds over her head and felt it rustle smoothly down over her shoulders. The peacock blue which on unwrapping the dress from its folds of tissue she had at first thought too intense a shade, she now realised did suit her perfectly, especially as she now had some colour in her cheeks from working out of doors in the spring sunshine.

Wearing her silver earrings and bracelet, the only jewellery she had, she felt quite glamorous. She used a little more make-up than usual, carefully applying the blue eye-shadow Amber had persuaded her to buy in Paris, and a new lipstick that was brighter than her usual choice of colour. The satin shoes went beautifully with the dress, such a good match they might well have been made of the same material.

Roland was in the hall when Louise reached the top of the stairs ready to go down, but she hesitated for a moment on seeing him, reluctant to confront him alone. He was standing with his back to her, obviously ready to leave. She stared at the back of his neck, trying not to let him disturb her. As she hesitated, Amber suddenly appeared below and walked across to Roland. Louise caught her breath. Amber looked absolutely stunning in the white and gold dress, with her blonde hair coiled in a classic Grecian style. She twirled in front of Roland.

'Well? How do I look?'

'Ravishing,' he smiled.

For a moment they stood motionless looking at each other, then Amber ran into his arms and buried her head against his shoulder. Her words, full of emotion, drifted up the stairs to the watching Louise.

'Oh, Roland, I try so hard not to mind, but ... the strain ... I can't wait for September to be over . . . is that awful? I feel so guilty . . .'

'Peter would understand,' he said softly, patting her shoulder.

She looked up at him. 'Yes, I know he would. Dear Peter! Of course he had it all worked out. He said he wouldn't mind a bit if I married you if he died . . .'

Louise turned swiftly and hurried back to her room. She could not bear to hear any more and she felt ashamed for having lingered long enough to hear so much. Trembling, she leaned against her bedroom door, trying to compose herself. There was no doubt now. She had heard them say it . . . Well, that should put a stop to any foolish feelings for Roland she had allowed to grow, once and for all. But she feared that it wouldn't. The sooner I finish what I have to do and leave here the better, she thought fiercely.

She waited five minutes and then ventured downstairs again. They were all waiting for her now, Amber and Roland, Philippa and Edgar, and Marie with the children, who had been allowed to stay up to see them go. As Louise descended the stairs she was aware of all their eyes on her, and especially Roland's, full of undisguised admiration. She would have felt flattered if it hadn't hurt so terribly.

Louise drove with Edgar in his car. Edgar remarked casually, as they set off, 'Roland is a bit dour, isn't he? Do you get along all right with him now?'

Louise had written to him briefly, at the beginning, of Roland's continuing opposition, but she had not told him exactly what had happened on her arrival.

'Quite well,' she said. 'He's just a bit moody.'

'He finally accepted your coming?'

'He had to really. It was a *fait accompli*.'

'He's a man who likes getting his own way, I fancy.'

'Exactly, but he doesn't always—at least not with Amber.'

They were following the Winterhaven car which now turned off the road into a long driveway leading to the d'Arbrisseau home, a small château, not unlike the Château des Ormeaux, but without towers and therefore of a more austere appearance. This, however, was softened by the moat which surrounded the building, and which now reflected it and all its lighted windows.

'What a delightful place,' said Louise, as they got out and went to join the rest of their party. 'I'd love to live in a château!'

'Perhaps you'll meet an eligible *comte* here tonight,' Edgar joked as he took her arm. 'I might have known my inheriting an art gallery and a farm wouldn't be enough for you!'

Louise smiled at him. 'You know perfectly well I wouldn't marry for money, and besides, you're not really in love with me.'

'I'm fond of you, though.'

'Love is something else. One day you'll find out and be glad I didn't take you seriously.'

'And you? You sound as though you've fallen in love yourself,' Edgar said shrewdly.

'Don't be silly,' said Louise. 'Who would I fall in love with here?'

They joined Amber, Roland and Philippa and crossed the forecourt together to the entrance to the château which was reached by crossing a drawbridge. Louise clung to Edgar's arm and resolved to stick

near him all night if she could. He spoke French a
lot better than she did.

This, however, proved easier said than done. As
soon as they arrived the General insisted on showing
them all the pictures that were to be in the exhibition.
Most were in one room, but others were in various
places throughout the château. After this quick tour,
Louise was commandeered by Madame d'Arbrisseau, who introduced her to various young people
in a room where there was music and dancing.
Abandoned here, Louise floundered a little, finding
conversation just a little wearying because of her lack
of French, so when she could she slipped away and
mingled with the rest of the party, smiling at everyone to give a good impression of enjoying herself, but
spending most of the time looking at the General's
pictures, of which there were many. He was certainly
an avid if rather indiscriminate collector, she decided.

Once through an open window she caught a
glimpse of Roland and Chantal walking along a terrace. Chantal stopped abruptly, her arms slid around
his neck and she raised her lips to his, Louise turned
abruptly away, feeling sorry for Amber. Did she
know what kind of man she was marrying?

She was admiring a large painting by Sisley when
Roland suddenly appeared at her side, without
Chantal.

'This was one of Peter's favourites,' he remarked.

'It must have hurt him terribly to have to part
with them.'

Roland's face was impassive. 'It did.' He sounded
almost as though he did not approve of the transac-
tion. Perhaps he thought the General had had the

best of the bargain. Roland went on, 'Where's Edgar? Not very gallant of him to neglect you.'

Louise shrugged. 'He's probably still discussing art with the General. And I'm enjoying myself. I've been dancing ...'

'I was about to ask if you would like to ... although I'm not much good at this modern stuff.'

'Neither am I, but Madame d'Arbrisseau introduced me to several people and they asked me to dance. I slipped away when I could.'

'To look for Edgar, I suppose. Louise, I didn't realise how close you were to Edgar Benson ... you should have mentioned it, and I wouldn't have ...'

'Kissed me,' Louise finished for him when he seemed loath to go on.

'I don't poach on other people's territory,' he said, and his tone reproached her for allowing it.

Louise decided it would be better if she did not enlighten him.

'Are you going to marry him?' Roland asked bluntly.

Louise hesitated only a second. 'He ... has asked me,' she answered truthfully.

Edgar chose that moment to join them, so Louise was saved further interrogation on that delicate matter.

'Ah, Roland, do you mind if I borrow Louise for a few minutes?' Edgar asked cheerfully.

'By all means ... she's all yours,' said Roland dryly.

Louise let Edgar steer her towards an open french window and on to the terrace. She sensed at once that something was wrong.

'Edgar, what's the matter?' she demanded.

He glanced around to make sure no one else was within earshot, then drew her closer. 'I think I'm going mad . . . seeing things!'

'What?' Louise was startled.

'The paintings, Louise . . . the ones that the General bought from Sir Peter Winterhaven, I just can't believe it . . . I'm totally at a loss.'

'For heaven's sake, Edgar, what are you getting at?' asked Louise impatiently.

'When I valued the paintings for Sir Peter I swear that every single one was a genuine original. I'd stake my life on it. But now . . . I'm convinced that all but two are fakes!'

Louise stared at him. It was the last thing she had expected him to say. All she could do was echo weakly, 'Fakes?'

CHAPTER EIGHT

THE reflections danced on the water of the moat and a light breeze ruffled Louise's hair as she continued to look incredulously at Edgar.

'Have you told him?' she asked at last.

'No. You can imagine what his reaction would be ... and besides, I keep telling myself I must be mistaken. How can they be?'

Louise slipped her arm through his. 'Could they have been fakes all along, and you were fooled the time before?' She added gently, 'It was several years ago ...'

He turned to her with an indignant exclamation. 'I wasn't fooled! I knew as much then as I do now. *I* sold Peter two of the paintings I now believe are fakes. And I'm sure they weren't when I sold them to him.'

Louise thought about it for a moment, then said, 'Well, it seems if what you believe is true, then someone has substituted copies for the originals.'

Edgar nodded agreement. 'Some very clever art thieves. The originals could easily be sold away from the mainstream of art dealers, because none of them are really well-known paintings, even the Sisley and the Cézanne wouldn't be well documented.' He paused, running his fingers through his hair agitatedly. 'How they managed to make the copies puzzles me, since you can't buy picture postcards of the General's collection!'

'Photographs?' suggested Louise.

'What else? Unless the General has loaned the pictures before, which I doubt.'

'Perhaps Sir Peter did,' suggested Louise.

Edgar shrugged. 'Possible. Anyway, speculation will get us nowhere. The point is, I now have to break the news to the General. He's as pleased as Punch about this exhibition. He doesn't know a lot about art, but he dearly wants to rank alongside important art collectors. It will be a terrible blow to his vanity.'

'Supposing you don't tell him until afterwards,' said Louise.

Edgar shook his head. 'Someone else might spot the fakes. Imagine the furore, the field day the newspapers would have. I'd be dragged into it. My reputation would be in question since it would be assumed I didn't spot the fakes. In any case, it would be a rotten trick to play on the General. He'd be made to look rather silly.'

'Art collectors and dealers have been made to look fools before,' pointed out Louise, 'and it's not as though he's going to sell any of them. It's only an exhibition.'

'No,' said Edgar firmly. 'I could be compromising my integrity not to reveal it.'

Louise squeezed his arm. 'Of course you would. I shouldn't have suggested such a thing. At least the General ought to be grateful to you for saving him the possibility of looking a fool. If he decides to go ahead regardless, then that's different.'

'I should advise him against it,' said Edgar. 'There's the question of the insurance, for one thing.'

'I still can't believe it,' said Louise. 'I was looking

at that Sisley for a quarter of an hour thinking how beautiful it was. It would never have crossed my mind ... well, I know I'm no expert, but surely they're extremely clever fakes?'

'Brilliant,' said Edgar grimly. 'Which makes one wonder how many others are around. I don't imagine the General has been the only victim. Unless I'm very much mistaken all were done by the same hand. I think that was what first alerted me, some common characteristic in the paintings of two quite different artists, which I'd never been aware of before. Oh, it's very subtle, and at first it was just a passing feeling, but when I began to take a second look at some of them, the awful possibility struck me.' He smoothed his hair again. 'Perhaps I'm wrong...'

'I doubt it,' said Louise. 'You know your job too well. The fakes might have fooled everyone else, but not you.'

'You're too kind,' Edgar remarked dryly. 'There are plenty of art experts sharper than I am, I assure you.'

'When are you going to give the General the bad news?' asked Louise.

'Not until I've had another closer examination and made a couple of tests. I can't do that tonight, naturally.' He smiled down at her. 'Come along, let's go back inside and imbibe some more of the General's excellent champagne. And remember, not a word to anyone!'

'As if I would!'

As they re-entered through the french windows, Louise saw Roland standing alone, looking rather morose. Edgar rushed off to find someone with a tray of champagne, leaving Louise with Roland.

'You're looking very radiant tonight,' he said. 'Edgar's coming has transformed you!'

'I expect my dress has more to do with any radiance than Edgar,' said Louise lightly. 'I've never owned such an exquisite gown, or one so expensive. Amber is just too generous . . .' She stopped, aware of his eyes roving over her bare shoulders, down her unadorned slender neck, to the shadowy crevice between her breasts. She added, 'And the champagne! It makes me feel quite lightheaded!'

His gaze returned to her face. 'Or perhaps it's . . . love?'

Louise felt her colour rising. There was nothing she could say except a flippant, 'Perhaps.'

Edgar returned with two glasses of champagne. 'Here you are, my sweet.' He handed one to Louise with a little bow and a wink, saying, 'Here's to us!' He glanced at Roland to include him, but Louise saw from Roland's rather stiff expression that he had interpreted it as an exclusively personal toast.

She said, 'To all of us!' but was not really anxious to correct any misapprehension.

Roland said, 'I think supper is being served. Shall we go and see?'

It was just after supper that Louise found herself for a few minutes alone with Chantal d'Arbrisseau. She took the opportunity to say how much she was enjoying the evening. Chantal dismissed the compliment airily, and then without any pretence at preliminary small talk, said bluntly:

'You are wasting your time chasing after Roland.'

Louise was taken aback. She opened her mouth, but could find no suitable rejoinder.

Chantal, smiling sweetly, had spoken as though

giving kind advice to a friend. Louise might have believed it had not the hard little downturn at the corner of the girl's mouth, and the jealousy in her eyes, betrayed her true motives.

'It is very embarrassing for him,' went on Chantal, with light laughter. 'Of course he cannot help being tall, dark and handsome, and physically attractive to women. But whatever you think, there is no future in it for you.'

'I'm sure I don't know what you're talking about,' said Louise defensively.

Chantal's mouth twisted disbelievingly. 'I am sure you do! I have noticed the way you look at him. You would like to get him into your bed.'

'How dare you!' Louise retorted hotly. 'I haven't the slightest interest in Roland Winterhaven. If anybody is trying to get him into her bed, it's you! And there's no future in that, surely, since he's going to marry Amber.'

It was Chantal's turn to look astonished. Clearly she had not expected so spirited a retort from Louise. She tossed her head haughtily, but there was uncertainty in her expression. 'That is only what the gossips say. I say he will not marry her.' She assumed a meaningful look, as she added, 'I am sure he will not. She is older than he is. She might think it would be very convenient, but he will not fall for that.' Her eyes narrowed, and she said determinedly, 'If anyone marries Roland, it will be me.'

'Well, it's none of my business whom he marries,' said Louise.

Chantal looked as though she half believed her. 'Monsieur Benson,' she said, 'he is your lover?'

The girl's frank questioning left Louise gasping,

but she controlled herself this time and answered cryptically, 'I think, Chantal, that my relationships, like Roland's, are my own business.'

Chantal laughed gaily. 'Well, I am sure I don't want to know all the boring little details! So long as you keep away from Roland.'

Louise, who felt that if she remained in the girl's company for very much longer she might say something she would regret, excused herself and went to find the powder room. There, looking in the mirror, she saw flushed cheeks and still flashing eyes, and her hands were trembling as she powdered her nose and combed her hair. The embarrassment of Chantal's youthful tactlessness, and the girl's abrasive manner, had disturbed her more than was necessary. She was angry with herself for feeling as she did now—jealous. Of Amber, and of Chantal.

'Don't be a fool,' she whispered emphatically. 'Don't be a stupid fool!'

Someone came in, so Louise hurriedly stuffed her make-up and comb back in her silver mesh purse and went back to find Edgar, wishing suddenly that it was over, and she did not have to look cheerful and as though she was enjoying herself for a minute longer.

The house was astir late the following morning. When Louise emerged she found she was first to come downstairs. She encountered Céleste, who was surprised to see her and said so.

'I thought you would want to sleep late,' the maid said, 'so I did not wake you this morning.' She smiled sunnily. 'You would like *le petit déjeuner* on the terrace? It is a beautiful morning. No wind.'

Louise agreed that it would be pleasant to eat outside, and while she was waiting, strolled leisurely up and down in the sunshine. Céleste soon reappeared with a tray which she set on a wrought iron table in a corner sheltered by rhododendrons.

Céleste questioned Louise eagerly about the party at the d'Arbrisseaux', and Louise endeavoured to give her a colourful description of the affair. Céleste sighed enviously, and Louise thought wryly that she might feel differently if she knew the problems that last night had thrown up.

When Céleste had gone, Louise lazily sipped her coffee and toyed with another delicious croissant, lavishly spreading butter and jam on it, while at the same time determining to eat less. Even the loose cotton shirt with smocked bodice and puff sleeves she was wearing over her jeans was a shade tight.

A procession of thoughts marched through her mind. She was dying to see Edgar, eager to know what further thought he had give to the business of the fake pictures. But it was not her uppermost thought. She could not banish the thoughts of Roland that perpetually intruded. Chantal's words kept coming back to her, and all at once she felt angry with him all over again. How dared he trifle with her feelings! First the harsh treatment, then disarming her with compliments and kisses, and all the time only playing with her because he could not help flirting with a woman, and finally having the cheek to reproach her over Edgar. She grimaced. It was no good blaming him. It was her fault. She should have maintained her dislike of him, not let herself fall victim to his insidious charm. If her emotions were topsy-turvy, there was no one to blame but herself.

She finished her breakfast and was about to return inside, to work, when Roland appeared. She had the immediate impression that he, as usual, had been up for hours. He joined her at the table and sat with one foot casually balanced across his other knee, tilting his chair back precariously as he looked at her.

'*Bonjour, mademoiselle*,' he said, with a faintly mocking smile. 'And how is the belle of the ball this morning?'

'If you mean Amber . . . or perhaps Chantal . . .?' she answered, wishing there had been no edge to her voice, 'I have no idea.'

He laughed softly. 'I mean you, *chérie*! What a pity you do not speak French more fluently. You would have heard some compliments to go to your head last night, I assure you.'

'Then perhaps it's just as well I don't,' Louise rejoined, feeling her face suffuse with colour, not because of what he was saying but because despite all her resolutions, he still had the power to set her senses on fire.

His gaze travelled slowly from the top of her sleek head down over her unmade-up face, her shapely body and slim legs to her small dainty feet in their flimsy sandals, and then back to her face, with faint amusement in his eyes at her discomfort.

'You look quite the *gamine* this morning, Louise, and you wear the look as well as you do that of the glamorous princess!'

She almost preferred his harsh treatment of her to this provoking manner.

'Isn't anybody else up yet?' she asked.

'Probably not. It was rather a late night. I'm surprised to see you up so early.'

'I always get up early ... well, mostly, anyway.'

He laughed. 'You'll make a good farmer's wife. Edgar was telling us about his farm in England.'

'Yes, it's in Wiltshire. It's a lovely place,' said Louise, implying, she realised, a greater intimacy with it than was actually the case. She had visited it once, and it had been Edgar's love of the country, to her at the time unexpected, that had made her think she might fall in love with him.

'But I suppose an artist really prefers the city,' Roland mused, 'the glamour of the galleries, and the personalities of the art world.'

Louise shook her head. 'Not at all. I should like very much to live in the country. I was born in a village, my grandparents were farmers, and the aunt who brought me up lives in the country in Scotland.'

He seemed surprised. 'I had imagined you with more sophisticated tastes.'

'Really?' She was genuinely surprised.

He studied her thoughtfully, 'Although, on reflection, perhaps the veneer is a little thin. Perhaps, in many ways, you're not always what you seem.'

Louise was anxious to escape, so she said briskly, getting up, 'I must get on with my work. So, if you'll excuse me ...' She added, 'If you see Edgar would you mind telling him I'm in the tower room?'

He nodded, and as she walked away she felt his eyes following her.

Louise did not see Edgar until lunchtime, and there was no opportunity then to discuss the fake pictures. The conversation at lunch was largely devoted to farming and gardening, once discussion of the previous night's party had been exhausted. Amber offered to show Edgar the garden during the afternoon and jokingly invited him to don a pair of gumboots and lend a hand. To Louise's surprise, Edgar agreed with alacrity. He also mentioned that he had arranged to go to see General d'Arbrisseau to assess the paintings and discuss the formal valuation for insurance purposes, the following day. Louise caught his eye and knew that the delay was already aggravating him.

'What are you going to do this afternoon, Louise?' asked Amber.

'Paint,' she answered.

'Will you need the children?'

'No, I don't think so. I can work without them at the moment.'

'Good,' said Philippa, 'I promised to take them out as consolation for not going to the party. There's a circus in Tours this afternoon.'

Louise painted for an hour after lunch, and then decided to make another effort to begin the portrait of Sir Peter Winterhaven. But, in spite of an initial rush of enthusiasm, it still would not come right. She thumbed through the photographs and press cuttings, and read bits at random in the biography, but without finding any inspiration.

'Perhaps it's because I can't put him in a heroic setting,' she thought at last, 'because I'm too young even to remember the war.'

She recalled suddenly that Amber had mentioned that there were many books in the library dealing with the Resistance movement, and World War II in general, so she decided to go down there and browse. Perhaps something would kindle a spark. It was worth a try.

Resolved, she cleaned her brushes and stood them

up in a jar, then ran downstairs. The house was still and cool and silent. The library blinds had been drawn against the morning sun, but as there was sufficient diffused light for her to see, Louise did not bother to raise them. She located the shelves where the books she wanted were, and browsed interestedly for a few minutes. Finally she selected a book she wanted to read, having found in it a reference to Sir Peter, and decided to take it back to the studio.

As she turned to go, something darted along the skirting board. It was dim at floor level, but she sensed it was a mouse running straight towards her. Instinctively she jumped to one side, but managed to catch one foot against the other and lock the buckles on her sandals. This caused her to stumble wildly. She clutched at the nearest projection which happened to be an ornate decoration in the panelling alongside the bookcase where she had been browsing. To her astonishment it gave under the pressure of her fingers, depressing into a small recess with a sharp click.

The panel it was attached to then moved. Louise's feet had become disentangled of their own accord, the mouse had vanished and was quite forgotten, as Louise, now intrigued, pushed the panel harder and saw it open like a door. Beyond there seemed to be a passageway. It was too dark to see more than a few paces into it.

Louise caught her breath. What a discovery! She stared into the darkness, all kinds of bizarre thoughts racing through her head. She wondered if Amber knew about it, or Roland, or had she discovered some mediaeval secret tunnel. She thrilled at the thought. There were probably dungeons down there . . .

Reluctant to pursue the discovery alone, she decided she must go and find someone to share it with. She reached into the gaping hole before her to pull the door to, and as she did so a hand closed over her other arm, and Roland's voice, behind her, said in quietly menacing tones:

'And where do you think you're going?'

CHAPTER NINE

As she turned to look at him, Louise's excitement faded. It was obvious he already knew of the secret passage and he was not at all pleased that she had discovered it.

'I . . . er . . . touched the panelling by accident. There was a mouse running across the floor . . . and I tripped and caught hold of that carved knob and it turned . . . and the door swung open.' She felt like a criminal caught safe-breaking.

He released her arm. 'You're a damn nuisance!' he snapped, with feeling, his eyes cold and grey as steel. 'You've done your level best to spoil everything, haven't you?' He glared at her. 'Well, now you'll have to know the truth, I suppose. If only you could have waited another few days, we might have . . .' He trailed off and grabbed her arm again. 'Come on.' He began to drag her through the opening into the passageway, at the same time flicking on a torch he had taken from his pocket.

Louise, frightened, tried to struggle. 'No! I'm not going down there with you. What's this all about?'

'You'll find out,' he answered her harshly.

Louise pulled back, but he was stronger. 'I'm not going to hurt you,' he rasped impatiently, 'I'm just going to show you something.'

'What?' She still resisted him.

'For goodness' sake, stop arguing, and come with me. Someone could come into the library at any minute and find us, and that's the last thing I want.'

'You mean no one else knows about the door?'

'No! Now are you coming or do I have to carry you?' He made a move to carry out the threat, but Louise hurriedly followed him into the passage, not wanting to suffer the same indignity she had suffered on the night of her arrival at the château.

Roland closed the door behind them, and Louise shuddered as she heard the lock click. She was alone with him now, with no idea of where he was taking her, or why. The beam of his torch lighted only a few feet in front of them. After a few yards Roland halted.

'Steps here ... watch out, there's nothing to hang on to and they're steep.'

He still had a tight grip on her hand, pulling her after him. Louise stumbled down what seemed an interminable stone staircase, which turned and twisted, until she was sure they must be right underneath the château. Immediately the thought of dungeons returned and she shivered. Roland did not speak, but she could hear his breathing, as no doubt he could hear hers.

Finally they stopped. The bottom of the staircase had been reached and now, over the musty smell, wafted a more familiar aroma of French cigarettes. Someone was smoking Gauloises. Louise guessed it was Henri since he almost invariably had one in his mouth whenever she encountered him. At the same time she recalled the day he had disappeared, when she had been sure he had gone into the library.

As she was thinking this they came to the end of a passageway and Roland stopped in front of what looked, in the gloom, like a door. A thin strip of light showed under it. The smell of Gauloises was stronger here.

Roland pulled the door open and a flood of electric light and warmer air rushed out. He pushed Louise into a room and closed the door. At first she was too blinded by the light, after the darkness of the passage, to be able to see anything, but in a moment it all came into focus and she gasped aloud.

There, hanging on the wall opposite her, was the Sisley painting she had admired for a quarter of an hour last night at the d'Arbrisseaux'. But how could it be ... She blinked, and slowly her gaze roved along the other walls. The room was a small art gallery, and there was the General's Cézanne ... and others ... all the paintings from Sir Peter Winterhaven's collection. She turned and looked at Roland for explanation, and his expression confirmed the devastating thought forming in her mind.

'You!' she whispered, incredulously. 'You're the one who stole the originals and replaced them with fakes ...' Suddenly the enormity of her discovery washed over her like a tidal wave. Roland! No, it couldn't be him. Roland couldn't be a thief ... she loved him. With a little sigh she slid into a crumpled heap on the floor.

When she came to she was lying on a camp bed in the same room. The pictures were still there. It was not a dream after all. Roland stood beside her, a glass in his hand. Henri Leveque hovered in the background.

'Here, have a sip of this.' Roland squatted by the bed and placed one hand behind her head to raise it, while the other held the glass to her lips. 'It's brandy.'

Louise noticed now that Henri was wearing a paint-spattered overall. Behind him was an easel with a half finished painting on it. Louise sipped the fiery liquid in the glass and pushed it away.

'I . . . I'm all right now.' she said shakily. 'It was just such a shock.'

Roland stood up, and looked down at her quizzically. 'You recognised the paintings as originals. That was very astute.'

Louise shook her head. 'No . . . I just knew the others were fakes. Edgar knows. He isn't sure yet . . . but he suspects.' Anguish rose up like bile in her. 'Roland . . . why? Why did you do it?' She sat up and grasped his hand. 'Why?'

He did not move, but turned his head slightly to speak to Henri. He spoke slowly and distinctly to the deaf old man and Louise was able to follow easily. 'I said Benson was no fool,' Roland said bitterly. 'Well, they've done for us now, Henri.'

Henri lifted his palms upwards in a despairing gesture.

'I didn't know Henri painted,' Louise said, her eyes straying to the easel. Many times he had stopped to watch her at work, standing silently behind her, but their conversation had been very limited. She said now, 'Did Henri do the fakes?'

Roland smiled. 'Yes. But he isn't a professional forger. He paints in his own right too and makes a few francs now and then for a landscape.' His expression became grim. 'Has Edgar told the general?'

'Not yet.'

Roland sat beside her on the bed, resting his chin in his hands, his elbows on his knees, in an attitude of utter dejection. Louise fought a desire to put her arm across his shoulders and comfort him. It was the last thing she should want to do.

Finally he turned to her and said, 'Things are not quite as they seem, Louise. I'd better tell you the story, and it's then up to you whether you believe it or not.'

'I can't believe . . .' Louise whispered, 'that you . . .'

He raised a hand to silence her. 'Listen, if you will, Louise. The truth is that Henri and I have not stolen the originals and replaced them with fakes. We've simply been trying to put the originals back.'

Louise's eyes opened wide and she gasped, 'Put them back!'

'Yes. Bizarre as that may sound to you, it's what we've been trying to do—what we've failed miserably to do, alas. It's a long story, but I'll try to be brief.

'Some years ago Sir Peter Winterhaven built up an enviable collection of paintings by some major, but mostly minor Impressionist and post-Impressionist painters. One of those who envied him was Raoul d'Arbrisseau. Peter hadn't a lot of time for him—all bluff and no brains, he used to say—but on the surface they were quite friendly. However, when the General refused to contribute to Peter's fund for a home for war veterans, but offered to buy the paintings so Peter could raise the money, Peter was disgusted with him. Unfortunately, in the end, in order to raise the money he needed, he was forced to accept the General's offer—a much lower one, I might add, than he might have got on the open market.'

'So why did he accept it?' asked Louise.

'So that he could keep his collection! Henri had

often demonstrated his copying skill during the war, forging passports and identity papers, but he was also a brilliant copyist of art works—without, I must add, ever trying to pass them off as originals. Henri isn't a criminal.'

Louise glanced at the Frenchman, immobile in the background, watching. A spiral of cigarette smoke curled to the ceiling.

Roland went on, 'In a few months Henri had copied all the pictures, working night and day down here. As soon as they were finished, Peter appeared to change his mind and offered them to the General. It must have given him great satisfaction to see the old fraud so easily defrauded!'

'It doesn't sound a bit like Peter Winterhaven to me,' interposed Louise suspiciously.

'No, I grant you, it doesn't fit the popular image, but it's true nonetheless.'

'And you knew all about the deception,' said Louise.

'Not until a few months ago, when I discovered by accident another entrance in the winery.'

'Doesn't even Amber know about the passage and this room?' Louise asked incredulously. 'Surely Sir Peter must have shown her.'

'Apparently not. I don't know why he didn't in the beginning—perhaps simply because it had been second nature to keep it secret when it was used to hide people during the war—and later, of course, he didn't because of the paintings. I was flabbergasted when I found them. Henri was still faithfully looking after them, and maintaining the air-conditioning which Peter had very cleverly installed and concealed.

'My first thought was to tell the General and return the originals, but I held back because I don't trust him. He's an egotist. I was afraid his chagrin at having been duped might persuade him to reveal the truth out of revenge, and I couldn't take such a risk . . .' He paused. 'It would break Amber . . .'

Amber, thought Louise dully. He loves her, so naturally he doesn't want her to be hurt.

'So,' Roland went on, 'I did nothing, but when the General decided to exhibit the paintings publicly, I was afraid some expert, like Edgar, would see they were fakes. There would be a ghastly scandal. You can imagine how the press would lap it up—a hero with feet of clay. Henri and I then agreed we must return the originals secretly. The d'Arbrisseaux were going to be away for several weeks, and conveniently it coincided with Amber's visit to London. We had plenty of time, we judged, to remove the fake pictures one by one, put the original canvases back in the frames, and replace them. Henri is not only an expert at such things but he has other talents and easily obtained a copy of a key to the château so we could come and go as we wished. We had only to worry about the couple of servants remaining at the château.'

'And Amber's sudden decision to have her children's portraits painted and to come back bringing me upset your plans,' Louise said, believing him now.

'Yes. I over-reacted, I'm afraid. You caught the brunt of it, and I'm sorry. I wasn't tactful enough with Amber either, and she dug her heels in.' He took a deep breath, then went on, 'I was desperately anxious that Amber should never suspect. I didn't want her image of Peter tarnished. He was a good man and what he did was not criminal . . . wrong, but not criminal, at least I don't think so.

'What he did was to let his love of art, his joy in possession of works of art which had taken years to collect, motivate him, also his need to complete his project, and his disgust over the General's meanness. It was justice to him. Nobody's perfect—and even heroes and saints act out of character sometimes. You can imagine what a big thing people would make of it if the story got out, especially with the dedication coming up. The spotlight would be on us with a vengeance.'

'You were taking a tremendous risk,' said Louise. 'You were risking your own for your uncle's reputation.'

Roland shrugged. 'He took risks many times for other people—much greater risks. He risked his life.' He added feelingly, 'He was always generous to me. He treated me as his son. I owe him some loyalty.'

Louise clasped her hands tightly together. She felt moved to tears, and she knew in that moment, if she had not known it before, how deeply she loved this man.

He said slowly, 'A scandal would harm a lot of people. I don't want Peter's friends, colleagues, all those who believe in him, hurt or disillusioned. Especially not Amber . . .' He paused. 'Especially not Amber,' he repeated. 'She's so—vulnerable.'

Louise flinched. It was so plain that he loved her dearly. That was what this was really all about. Roland had been willing to take the risk as much for Amber as for her dead husband.

'Edgar says he thinks two of the pictures are originals,' she said.

'All we've managed to replace!' said Roland grimly, then he smiled. 'You almost caught us at it twice—once that night you went walking in the moonlight, and once when you wandered into the winery. We were smuggling the pictures out through the winery. There's a narrow tunnel that comes up there and we decided to use it instead of risking being seen in the château, even in the dead of night. I was sure you were suspicious. I'd become quite paranoid about it, I can tell you!'

'But I'd never have guessed in a million years!' exclaimed Louise.

'I was terrified you'd talk to Amber if you saw anything odd and she'd start asking questions. I was as jumpy as a rookie burglar! I'm not very good at criminal activities.'

He was making a joke of it, but Louise knew now how serious it was. 'I'm sorry my coming here spoilt things,' she said.

Roland looked at her without rancour. 'When you refused to co-operate, we decided we'd just have to go through with it and hope for the best.'

'You could have told me what you were doing,' she reproached.

'Could I? I didn't know you. I didn't know how you would view it. Several times I was tempted to, but I decided it was best for no one except Henri and me to know.'

'The d'Arbrisseaux coming back must have made it doubly difficult,' said Louise.

Roland grimaced. 'And how! We tried operating right under their noses, but Chantal has this damned lapdog that roams the château at night and barks if it sees its own shadow. Henri and I decided to bide our time, hoping they'll soon go off to Cannes, leaving us enough time before the Paris exhibition to finish the changeover. But now that Edgar knows . . .'

Louise, remembering Edgar's words, said, 'Edgar assumes that a very clever gang of art thieves is responsible. He's afraid other collectors may have suffered in the same way.'

'The General won't believe that,' said Roland flatly. 'He'll suspect Peter right away.'

'But there's no proof.'

'Suspicion will be enough,' said Roland grimly. 'And if jealousy fires suspicion, as I expect it will—the General is very jealous of all the fuss being made of Peter posthumously, since after all he played a part in the war too—he may want to destroy Peter simply out of revenge. He's been made a fool of and he won't like it.'

Silence fell in the room. Louise looked from one picture to the other, still unable to take in all that Roland had told her, but convinced now that he was telling the truth. He sat morosely on the end of the camp bed, his shoulders slumped, utterly defeated, and she wished she knew how to help him. She loved him and it hurt to know that he loved another, but still she had to try and help him.

The answer came to her as a flash of inspiration. She said, 'The General doesn't know yet that his pictures are fakes. Edgar isn't going to see him until tomorrow.'

'He'll tell him then. What difference does that make? We've no hope of replacing them all before then. We shall just have to tell the truth. The originals are legally the General's—and morally. I couldn't keep them.'

'Edgar might be persuaded not to tell him,' said Louise.

Roland looked up sharply. 'Not to tell him? But . . .'

'I think Edgar could be persuaded to help us,' she said. 'I'm sure he'll see that there are very good reasons.'

Roland sighed. 'But there's still the risk that another expert will realise the truth, and then where would Edgar be? He won't compromise himself by valuing them as originals when he knows they're not.' He stopped, then said slowly, 'but if he was prepared to and we could complete the changeover after they go to Cannes . . . no, that would be too risky. Edgar would be a fool to agree.'

'I've got a better idea,' said Louise confidently. 'Supposing Edgar persuades the General to part with the collection to him for some reason—say for cleaning and stretching and that sort of thing—then he'd be able to take the pictures away, and when they're returned, you'll have substituted the originals. The General will be keen to have his pictures in prime condition, I'm sure, and Edgar is after all an expert.'

An expression of wonder came over Roland's face. 'You mean you're prepared to try and persuade Edgar?'

'I can try.'

'Why?' His eyes searched her face.

Louise looked away. 'I wouldn't want Amber to be hurt either. As you said, nobody's perfect, and I'm rather glad to find that Sir Peter wasn't. Besides, I have a commission to paint his portrait. I don't want to lose it because he's been unmasked.'

He regarded her thoughtfully, 'And Edgar, of course, will do anything for you.'

She smiled at him. 'I hope so!'

She stood up and walked a few paces away, feeling shaky. Roland came up to her and put his arm around her shoulders. He looked down into her face. 'Louise, I don't know how I shall ever be able to thank you.'

'Let's see whether it works first.' Louise said matter-of-factly. 'Now, hadn't I better be getting back before someone misses me?'

But Roland did not move. He bent his head lower. 'My dear girl,' he said softly, and kissed her.

She did not mean to, but her lips responded to his of their own accord. She could not help it, even though she knew his kiss was only out of gratitude and that all his love was for Amber.

'You're looking rather flushed,' said Edgar, when he met Louise, as she was about to go upstairs. 'Somebody been kissing you?'

'No!'

His arm dropped lightly across her shoulders. 'Then somebody should!' He kissed her cheek lightly, and at the same moment Roland appeared, having left the library a moment or two after Louise. Louise drew back from Edgar, but knew Roland had seen him kissing her. It didn't matter, she thought, that he was convinced they were in love. That was better than his guessing her true feelings.

'I hope you had a pleasant morning, Edgar,' Roland remarked affably.

'Very pleasant,' Edgar answered. 'Amber has fully persuaded me that I'm a true son of the soil!' He put a hand to his back and grimaced. 'I used to be content just to look at the garden and let someone else do all the work. I'm not as fit as I thought and she's a hard taskmistress. However, one can never refuse a beautiful woman anything, can one?'

A guarded look came into Roland's eyes and Louise suspected that he was mildly jealous. In spite of what he believed about her and Edgar, he was jealous because Edgar had been enjoying himself in Amber's company all morning.

Roland said, 'They do have a way with them, I grant you.' He exchanged a glance with Louise, his half conspiratorial, half flirtatious.

He went on ahead of them up the stairs and as he disappeared and they followed more slowly, Edgar remarked, 'He seems a bit uptight about something. Maybe he's jealous because I kissed you!'

'Hardly!' retorted Louise. She caught hold of his arm. 'Edgar, I've got to talk to you urgently—and privately.'

His eyebrows rose. 'What about?'

'I can't tell you now. It'll take a little time.'

Edgar naturally looked perplexed. 'This is very intriguing.'

'Edgar, you haven't said anything to Amber about the fake pictures, have you?' Louise asked anxiously.

'No. I don't want to commit myself until I'm positive.'

Louise was relieved. 'Good. It's terribly important that you don't.'

'Why?'

'I can't explain now,' she said. 'Later.'

Presently, as they went in to lunch, Edgar was ahead talking animatedly to Amber, and Roland hung back a little with Louise. Philippa had not joined them yet, so as he bent his head close to

Louise, he was able to say, 'Have you approached him yet?'

'I haven't had a chance. There was no time before lunch. Tonight after dinner I'll try and do it.'

Roland looked disappointed and Louise felt a rush of sympathy for him. She had given him hope when he had thought all hope was lost, and she knew he was banking on Edgar's co-operating. Without thinking she felt for and pressed his hand. 'It'll be all right,' she said. 'I'm sure it will. Edgar is a reasonable man.'

He managed a smile. 'Would you marry any but a reasonable man? I'm sure he is.' His fingers tightened around hers. 'And as he said, who can resist the pleas of a beautiful woman!'

Greatly though Louise desired to have Edgar to herself that evening, the opportunity did not arise. After dinner he ensconced himself very firmly in the drawing room playing chess with Amber, who, when Edgar had remarked on the exquisite craftsmanship of the antique chess set in that room, had invited him to play with her.

'You'll beat me,' she told him gaily. 'I'm too flighty, as Roland would say, to concentrate on clever moves. Peter tried to teach me, but I wasn't a very good pupil.'

'Perhaps I can succeed where he failed,' commented Edgar with a teasing smile.

Later, when Edgar reminded her of her invitation to play, she had glanced at the others. 'You don't mind?'

Assured that nobody did, after dinner Amber and Edgar sat down at the chess table. Soon afterwards Philippa excused herself saying she wanted to write a couple of letters, and so Louise was left alone with Roland. They made desultory conversation for some time, both uncomfortably aware that the subject uppermost in both their minds could not be discussed, and both on edge because Louise was unable to get Edgar alone.

Finally, when she could see that any hope of talking to Edgar that night was fast fading, and because sitting alone with Roland, making small talk, put her on edge for other reasons, Louise decided she might as well go to bed.

When she quietly rose and said good night, Amber tried to dissuade her, with apologies for neglecting them, and said she and Edgar would not play another move. Roland intervened.

'I've got a few things to do in the office,' he said, 'so if Louise wants to retire, you two might as well continue your game. It seems to be an absorbing one.'

Louise darted a quick glance at him, feeling sure she detected a trace of irritation in his tone. He confirmed it when, as they were bidding each other good night at the foot of the stairs, he said, 'You don't seem to mind Edgar flirting with Amber.'

It was obvious that he minded very much. Louise could only shrug. 'I don't think Amber has any designs on Edgar.'

'You're very trusting.'

Louise was loath to continue the discussion, so she quickly murmured good night and hurried up the stairs.

The next morning Louise finally managed to see Edgar alone. He was apologetic about the previous evening.

'I couldn't refuse to play with her, could I?'

They were strolling in the garden, and Louise suggested they walk towards the lake. There was a seat there where they could talk without fear of being overheard. She could not help saying, 'I think you made Roland a bit jealous, though.'

'I wasn't flirting,' Edgar replied indignantly. 'If anyone was, it was Amber!' He added archly. 'Perhaps you were a bit jealous, too?'

'Edgar!' Louise said warningly.

He tucked her arm through his. 'All right, I give up. I won't pester you any more. Now what's all this mystery about?'

They sat down. The air was still and a strong perfume of flowers drifted across from the beds near the house. Beyond the lake the woods were in full leaf and above hung the soft powder blue panoply of the sky.

Louise took a deep breath and announced, 'I've found the original paintings.'

Edgar jerked round to face her. 'What did you say?'

Louise couldn't help a smile. Edgar looked as though his eyeballs were about to pop out. A dubious look came into his face. 'You're pulling my leg.'

'No, it's true. I want you to listen while I tell you the whole story. I don't want you to make any judgements until I've finished.'

Edgar listened attentively to her, without interruption. When she came to the end of her story, he was silent for some moments, before he said, 'Well, that's about the most bizarre story I've heard in a long while, and if you hadn't told me it, I wouldn't have believed it. Peter Winterhaven a crook!'

'He wasn't!' Louise defended. 'He can surely be

forgiven for what he did. It wasn't criminal . . . well, not really.' She caught hold of Edgar's sleeve. 'Edgar, if the truth comes out, think of what it will do to all those involved—and especially Amber.'

Edgar's face was grim. 'What do you propose we do?'

This was the hard part. Louise bit her lip. 'I . . I have a plan. I hope you'll co-operate.'

'I'm not getting involved in anything shady,' said Edgar primly.

'It won't be . . . very shady,' promised Louise. She went on to explain what his part in the substitution would be, finishing with a plea. 'It's just a little subterfuge to put right what must be put right. There's no other way to do it without hurting people. Please, Edgar . . . it would destroy Amber to discover the truth.'

Edgar pulled his chin thoughtfully. 'Amber . . . yes, you're right, it probably would,' he murmured. 'Especially right now, with all this dedication fuss and palaver coming up, and the biography . . . yes, it would upset her terribly. She idolised the man. It would be very humiliating for her and the children . . .'

Louise was slowly letting out a deep sigh of relief. He was more sympathetic than she had dared to hope. Like Roland, like herself, he didn't want Amber to be hurt.

Finally Edgar shook his head, bemused. 'I can't believe it—Peter! He took a hell of a chance, Louise. Somebody could have spotted that those paintings were fakes while he was still alive.'

'He might have insisted he'd been fooled himself.'

'Hardly. His collection came from a dozen different sources. They couldn't have all been fakes.'

'Well, what about your art thieves theory?'

'Mmm, but that's pretty far-fetched if you think about it. No, Peter certainly took a calculated risk.'

'Which he'd been doing most of his life,' Louise reminded him. 'Even on the day he died.'

'He could always have seen his pictures at the General's,' said Edgar. 'It's not as though they went far.'

Louise snorted. 'What about pride? No, Edgar, for him this was the only way. I don't think we should delve into his motives too deeply in any case. He was a hero, there's no doubt of that, and that's an image worth preserving, isn't it? We haven't the right to destroy that image just because we've discovered a weakness.'

Edgar regarded her shrewdly. 'Roland has been very convincing.'

'His plan might have succeeded, but for me.'

'What nonsense!' scoffed Edgar. His look was thoughtfully searching. 'I get the feeling you'd do almost anything to please Roland.'

Louise felt her colour rising. 'It isn't for him . . .'

'No? There's been something different about you, Louise, ever since I arrived. I believe you're in love.'

'Of course I'm not! Is it so odd to want to see somebody you like very much, as I like Amber, protected?'

'All right, I believe you,' soothed Edgar with a smile. 'And I'll go along with your plan, but don't forget, it might not work.'

Louise smiled her most encouraging smile. 'I feel sure it will.'

Louise painted during the remainder of the morning, and in the afternoon when Edgar drove over to the General's, she was again in the tower studio working hard on the portrait of Sir Peter. It was only a preliminary sketch, but for the first time her brush worked with a fluency she had not been able to achieve before in her attempts to portray the man.

Once or twice, standing back to look critically at her work, she mused idly, as she so often had, on the extraordinary alchemy that was painting. All she was doing was filling a brush with pigment and applying it to canvas according to recognisable techniques, and so why did it work sometimes, at others fail? It was still a mystery to her.

'Forget the mysteries and just paint,' Edgar had always said, 'from the heart!'

Louise sighed. Edgar had done so much for her, been her mentor for so long, it seemed ungrateful not to repay him by marrying him. And that was another mystery. She respected and admired him, was genuinely fond of him, yet knew deep in her heart that she did not love him as a woman ought to love the man she married.

Late in the afternoon there was a tap at the door and when Louise called, 'Come in!' and turned eagerly, expecting Edgar to have returned, she saw Roland standing there.

'Am I interrupting?' He paused uncertainly, glancing around the room. 'I thought Edgar might be back.'

Louise, palette and brush still poised, was struck dumb by a rush of emotion. She wanted to fly into his arms and tell him that everything was going to work out fine, but she just stood there, stupidly speechless.

At last she found her voice. 'No . . . as you can see, he isn't. He said he'd come straight up.'

Roland did not then go as she expected. He came

further into the room and she was immediately reminded of her first night at the château when he had dragged her struggling, over his shoulder, into this room, and she had been certain he meant to rape her. Her face warmed at the recollection, but she felt no resentment. She knew that he was not really a violent man, that in a desperate situation he had been driven to desperate measures.

He looked at her lengthily now, a smile slowly forming on his firm but sensuous mouth. He was remembering too, she felt sure. At last he said, 'I hope you've finally forgiven me for my brutal treatment of you when you first arrived. It was unforgivable, but . . .'

'It's a pity I was so stubborn,' she answered.

He crossed to her easel and studied the sketch for some moments. Then he said admiringly, 'That's terrific, Louise. That's Peter all right.' His smile became a reminiscent grin. 'You've captured something . . . some elusive expression, difficult to pinpoint, but that wayward child look he sometimes had. How could you know . . .?' He looked at her wonderingly. 'And with only photographs to go on.'

'It's only a preliminary sketch,' said Louise, studying the canvas critically herself, and wondering how she did know.

'I'll look forward to seeing the finished portrait,' he said, adding, 'Amber is delighted with the pictures of the children. So am I. You seem to have a magic touch.'

'Thank you.'

He laughed. 'I admire your patience. It must be very frustrating trying to paint continuously moving objects!'

'Oh, they sit still for me sometimes. They're quite good really. Actually Selena is showing quite a bit of artistic talent herself. Would you like to see some sketches she made the other day?' As their prospective stepfather, she thought, he ought to be made aware of any talents in his new family.

Louise was also glad of something to divert him from her work, and herself. Standing so close to him, she had this silly desire to take him in her arms. She rushed over to a portfolio lying on a chair and fetched out the sketches. They discussed them for a few minutes, and finally he asked, 'Have you shown them to Amber?'

'Yes. She was quite surprised. She said she would speak to you about art classes.' A silence fell, the subject was exhausted, and Louise nervously glanced at her watch. 'I wonder how much longer Edgar will be.'

Roland did not answer but brushed her cheek with the tip of his forefinger. She drew back.

'You just put a dab of paint on your cheek,' he said teasingly. He picked up a rag and wiped it off properly, while Louise stood rigidly, allowing him to do it, and fighting the desire to fall into his arms.

She laughed a little shakily. 'I get covered in paint daily!' She indicated her paint-spattered smock. 'I'm a very messy worker.'

'And I'm wasting your time,' he apologised, dropping the rag back over the rung of her stool. He considered her for a moment and then asked, 'How much longer will you need to be here?'

'I was thinking I might go back when Edgar does,' Louise said, voicing the idea that had been in her mind all day. 'I can finish the portraits in my own studio. Amber and the children will be coming over to London and we can have a final sitting then. She will also have to approve the finished portrait of Sir Peter.'

'Well, I'd better let you get on,' said Roland.

Louise did not want him there, disturbing her composure, but she didn't want him to go either. She said, 'The light's fading now. I shan't do any more today. Sit down and wait for Edgar if you like. I'm sure he won't be long.'

Roland did not demur. He sat on the edge of the divan, hands clasped between his knees, and suddenly Louise could think of nothing to say to him. She busied herself tidying up her paints, and cleaning her brushes, as the dusk deepened in the room. Roland seemed too preoccupied for conversation.

Finally there was a tap at the door and both of them jumped.

'Come in!' Louise called.

Edgar slipped quietly into the studio. 'What's up? Lights fused, or a power cut?' he enquired cheerfully.

'No . . . I mean . . .' Louise was stupidly confused.

'Then why are you sitting in the dark?' He saw Roland for the first time. 'Ah . . . Roland, I didn't see you there.'

'We were talking,' Louise explained quickly. 'And we didn't notice it was getting dark.'

Edgar looked from one to the other. 'No, I suppose not.'

Roland got up and switched on the light. Louise asked, 'Well, what happened, Edgar?'

He sat down on the divan while Roland remained standing. His face gave nothing away and it was a long moment before he spoke. Then he looked at Louise, smiled broadly, and said,

'It worked!'

Everyone else had gone to bed, but Louise was restless, so, still fully dressed, since she knew she would never sleep if she went to bed, she went downstairs and slipped outside. She walked slowly down towards the lake. It was moonlight and the shimmering water gleamed silver as a slight breeze ruffled its mirror surface. A frog croaked and a duck suddenly squawked and fluttered through the dark clumps of reeds.

Louise stared at the water, thinking that soon it would all be over and she would be going home with Edgar. There was a strange tugging at her heart as she thought of it.

He came up to her so quietly that she did not notice him until he touched her arm. She jumped. 'Roland!'

'Sleepless too?' he murmured.

'It it any wonder?'

'No regrets?' he asked.

She was startled. 'No, why should I?'

He shrugged. 'I'm very grateful, Louise.'

'There's no need.' She felt uncomfortable.

He looked hard at her. 'You know you're not at all the girl I first thought you were, sitting there so timidly in Amber's mother's apartment in London, overawed and clearly rather nervous. I thought you were a pushover then . . .'

'I was . . .'

'I expected you to be later too, but you turned out to be someone else altogether then, bold and worldly . . . and yet you often seem nervous and afraid,

very unsure of yourself . . . although you can be as
stubborn as a mule and rise to a challenge like no
one I know. I really don't know what to make of
you, Louise.'

'I'm not sure what to make of myself sometimes,'
she said, with a light laugh.

'This commission means a lot to you, doesn't it?'
he said.

'It's my first real one.'

'Really? But I had the impression from Edgar . . .'

'Oh, he boosts my ego no end. It's very sweet of
him, I suppose. He says what I'd never dare to say
myself.'

'No wonder you're in love with him,' commented
Roland.

Louise did not answer. The breeze suddenly felt
chill to her. She shivered. 'It's cooler than I thought.
I think I'd better go in.'

Roland fell into step beside her and they walked
in silence back to the house. He offered her a night-
cap, 'To help you sleep,' and she could think of no
reason not to go with him into the drawing room
and sip a sherry while he had a whisky. It was a little
less disconcerting being with him there than out in
the moonlight.

They talked for a time about Edgar's plan to
remove all the paintings for cleaning and re-stretch-
ing, which the General had agreed to surprisingly
readily, and the plan to replace the fakes with the
originals. Finally Louise yawned.

'I'd better be off to bed. It's nearly morning!'

'I think I'll just have another,' said Roland.

Louise turned to go. 'Good night, Roland.'

His hands dropped on to her shoulders and turned

her around to face him. There was a strangely intense look in his eyes as he said softly, 'I want you to know that I shall never forget what you did.'

She felt the tears coming unexpectedly into her eyes. 'I did . . . nothing.'

His lips touched hers briefly, and he smiled. 'You know, if it wasn't for Edgar . . .' He pushed her gently away. 'Go on, off to bed!'

Louise went, thinking bleakly that what he had really meant was, '. . . if it wasn't for Amber . . .'

CHAPTER TEN

THE day the invitation came, Louise was working on
a portrait which she was eager to finish, so she did
not stop to look at her mail until the evening. She
had been working hard since her return from France.
Several commissions had resulted from her exhibition
at the Profile Gallery in the spring and Amber
Winterhaven had been the source of at least a few
others.

Louise had been delighted and not a little surprised. She had tended to regard the Winterhaven
commission as a bit of a fluke, despite Edgar's re-
assurances, and had half expected to be looking for a
job in a commercial art studio before very long. But
her pessimism was not justified and she had plenty of
work to occupy her for some months. She was also
able to move into a more workmanlike studio, with
flat attached, which pleased her enormously. She
began to feel that she had really 'arrived'.

She was also glad of plenty of work as it kept her
mind occupied, for most of the time at least. But she
could not work all the time, and there were periods,
especially in the evenings, when her mind would drift
back, remembering those weeks in France, and
Roland . . .

At the last minute everything had happened quite
swiftly. When General d'Arbrisseau had agreed to
let Edgar take the paintings that were to be exhibited
in Paris away for cleaning and other restorative attention, Edgar had acted without delay in case he

changed his mind. Louise smiled, recalling Edgar's devious strategy.

'I told him I knew a good man in Paris,' Edgar had told them afterwards, 'but that rather than give him the trouble of transporting the pictures there, I would personally supervise it, since I was in the vicinity, and make sure they received the very best attention. He was a bit reluctant at first, but I assured him that if he was not to court criticism for carelessness, the work was essential. He bought it, thank goodness.' He had laughed. 'He cares very much about his image as an art collector!'

Louise was anxious to know what would happen to the fakes.

'They'll have to be destroyed,' Edgar had insisted. 'I shan't take part in this unless they are. We can't risk someone getting hold of them at some other time.'

'Poor Henri,' Louise had said sadly. 'All that work for nothing.'

Roland had interposed, 'Not for nothing. He did it for Peter. He knows it must happen. We were going to destroy them.' He had placed a comforting hand on Louise's shoulder. 'Don't fret, Louise—Henri won't.' He had smiled reassuringly at her, and she had felt rather foolish.

At first there had seemed to be a stumbling block. How was the switch to be made without anyone else becoming involved in the deception? Edgar, fully committed now, eventually provided the solution, which proved to be a simple one. He had a friend in Paris who owned a studio apartment.

'If he's not using it at the moment, I shall ask him to lend it to me,' Edgar had said, and had winked at Roland. 'Being French he'll never guess the real reason!'

Luck had stayed with them. Edgar's friend had co-operated willingly. There had then remained only the problem of getting the original canvases from the secret room to the studio in Paris, and making the switch.

This had proved fairly easy to accomplish, since without their frames, the paintings could be packed into quite a small container. This was smuggled out into Edgar's station wagon. The fake pictures were collected by a special van from the General's, under Edgar's strict supervision. Edgar and Henri were to switch the paintings over in Paris and then transport them on to the restorers. Henri's excuse for going to Paris was that he needed to see an eye specialist. Amber did not for one moment question his trip.

They had all left together, the van, Edgar with Henri, and Louise in her own car. Louise sighed as she recalled the moment of departure. It had been a heartbreaking moment.

'We've loved having you, Louise,' Amber had said, pressing her hand warmly and kissing her. 'We really have, and you must come and stay with us again . . . but just as a friend next time. Will you? We get on so well together.'

Louise had promised she would, but looking at them standing there together, Amber and Roland, with the children around them, she had felt that it would be too painful. Somehow she would have to find an excuse if Amber ever did invite her.

Parting with the children had been difficult too, because she had become very fond of them in the few weeks she had been painting them. She envied Philippa her continuing life at the château, in a way, but knew she would not really change places with her even if it were possible, because it would be too painful.

Parting from Roland had been the worst. She had wished she could just vanish and not have to say goodbye, but that was impossible. She had avoided last-minute moments alone with him, so it was with everyone else standing around that she said a formal goodbye before getting into her car.

He took her two hands in his, kissed her lightly on the cheek, and said, 'Thank you for everything, Louise ... I wish you every happiness for the future, and I hope you'll remember me more kindly than I deserve.'

Tears had started in her eyes. All she could say, tremulously, was, 'G-goodbye, Roland. I ... I don't think badly of you. I wish you happiness too.' She glanced at Amber, but Amber was talking animatedly to Edgar, and did not hear the exchange.

Roland dropped a last kiss on her forehead and whispered, 'And don't worry, you *will* be paid for the portraits!'

Louise looked up into his teasing eyes and her tears almost flowed over. Fortunately, at that moment little Angela came rushing up and pushed a bunch of flowers into her hands. The distraction was enough to disguise her sudden upsurge of emotion and allow her to take a hold on herself.

Then both she and Edgar had got into their cars and with a last shouted farewell and waves, had left. Louise had been glad to be driving alone, and as they passed swiftly through the soft misty landscape of the Loire Valley, she knew she was imprinting on her mind for ever the vineyards, the fields, the woods, the meandering river and its tributaries, the clouds and the powder blue sky. And on it, like a transparent overlay, would be the faces of the people she had left behind, and especially one dear face . . .

Henri was staying with friends in Paris, so as there was only one bed in the studio flat, Louise checked into a hotel, musing to herself that Roland almost certainly believed she would be staying with Edgar.

When the job was done and the paintings delivered to the restorers, just to keep the record straight, although very little work was needed on them, Edgar took Louise out to a celebratory dinner and the opera. They drank champagne and toasted the success of the enterprise, and also her success in her first commission as a portrait painter. But both were rather subdued and preoccupied. Louise guessed that Edgar might be having some private misgivings about his role in the affair.

And he had not, Louise reflected now, as she tidied her palette and brushes, once mentioned marriage, either then or since. He had finally accepted her view of their relationship, it seemed.

In the weeks immediately after their return to England, Louise had thrown herself wholeheartedly into finishing the portraits of the Winterhaven children, and in completing the portrait of Sir Peter. At the end, when she felt she could do no more, she suffered one of her customary bouts of diminished confidence, looking at her work with a deep sense of failure, but Edgar, as usual, restored her confidence by praising her work highly, and from him she had to accept it. He was an expert and he did not flatter.

'You've got a future,' he told her generously, 'and not just painting children to please their mamas.

Your portrait of Peter shows you've got depth. It's a
fine work, Louise.'

She had been pleased with his assessment, but still
a little anxious about Amber's reaction. She need
not have worried. Amber gave her wholehearted
approval to all the paintings, and was especially
thrilled with the portrait of her late husband.

She stayed in London for a few weeks, to make up,
she told Louise, for her rather brief stay earlier in the
year. Louise met her once or twice at the Profile
Gallery, and they had lunch together once with
Edgar, but she did not see Roland. He was busy,
Amber said. There was a lot to do on the estate
during summer.

'You'll have to come back for the vintage,' she
said gaily, 'and of course the dedication.'

Louise scarcely had time to think much about it.
The paintings were finished and despatched. Edgar
offered to go and hang them for Amber, and to advise
on the framing of the portrait of Sir Peter. He was
also, he told Louise, with a twinkle, going to see the
exhibition of General d'Arbrisseau's collection in
Paris.

As the weeks passed, Louise's spring sojourn
gradually began to fade into the realms of dreams
and memories. Only Roland still haunted her
dreams, and sometimes she regretted not having even
one sketch of him. She had destroyed the only one
she had made at the château. Sometimes she would
try to capture his features from memory, but they
always eluded her and she either made him look like
a gargoyle or a pop star.

Having tidied the studio and returned to her flat,
Louise at last looked through her mail. She turned

the invitation over in her hand. It looked like a
wedding invitation, she thought, looking at the crisp
white parchment envelope, and her heart missed a
beat. It could only be Roland and Amber . . .

But it was not a wedding invitation. It was her
invitation to the dedication ceremony of the memorial to Sir Peter Winterhaven in Les Deux Croix.

'I can't go,' Louise thought, covering her face
with her hands. 'He'll be there . . . with her. I can't
go . . .'

The telephone rang. It was Edgar. 'You've had
your invitation?' he demanded at once.

'Yes, I only just opened it. I was busy all day, and
didn't get around to looking at my mail before.'

'Same here. We'll go together, of course.' Edgar
sounded quite excited about it.

Louise knew it would be impossible to get out of
going. Edgar would demolish any excuses she offered,
and she did not want him to realise the truth. He
had come near to suspecting her feelings a couple of
times while they were in France. Afterwards she
consoled herself with the thought that there would
be hundreds of people there, so she could lose herself
in the crowd. It was Amber's accompanying letter,
however, which dismayed her most. Amber wanted
her to stay at the château. She could scarcely refuse,
but half of her dreaded it, and half of her knew it
would be wonderful to see Roland again, if only
briefly.

At the dedication of the Sir Peter Winterhaven
memorial, Louise was not just one of the crowd as
she had hoped. As the artist who had painted the
portrait of the hero, she was amongst the very im-

portant guests and was obliged to sit on a dais with Amber and the children and Roland, as well as a host of local dignitaries and other people involved.

The village was *en fête* for the occasion, with the Town Hall, churches and every house flying flags and bunting. But the dedication service was serious and meaningful, and Louise was able to follow most of what was said. She saw out of the corner of her eye, Amber wiping away a tear, and she felt a sudden rush of gladness that Peter had not been exposed. She caught Roland's eye and for a moment they shared each other's thoughts. He was offering a silent prayer of gratitude too, she knew.

Afterwards there was celebrating of a less serious nature, and Louise was whirled from one group of people to another, being constantly congratulated on her portrait. She managed to survive with her faltering French and winning smile, although she found the ordeal exhausting. She was glad when all the formalities were over and they returned to the château.

'I think I'm going to have one of my headaches,' said Amber, looking rather pale, as she and Louise were going upstairs together.

'Is there anything I can get for you?' Louise asked solicitously.

Amber gave her a long, rather apprehensive look. 'No . . . but I'd like you to come and talk to me in a few minutes, just as soon as you're ready. I want to talk to you—privately.' She looked uneasy, and Louise wondered why. What could she want to say to her?

Louise was in her old room. The first thing she did was to walk to the window and look out. She sighed with nostalgia. She had only lived here for a few weeks in spring, but she had felt a real part of it. She looked down towards the lake and across the sweeping vineyards to the distant hills, and she felt a sharp pang of regret that she was but a passing figure in the landscape.

As she was staring bleakly out of the window, a figure came into view. Roland strolled alone down to the lake, his hands clasped behind his back. He stood gazing into the still water, a picture of utter dejection, and Louise frowned. Why should he look so sad? Her heart ached, and yet she could not take her eyes from the solitary figure who surely now, that the past was settled and safe, could resolve the future. When he turned and started to walk back, saw her, and raised a hand in greeting, Louise felt her heart must break. All the intervening weeks had made no difference to her feelings at all.

She pulled herself together and went along to Amber's room. Amber was lying on the bed, with the shutters closed, and in the half dark Louise thought she was asleep.

'Come in, Louise,' the figure on the bed called as she hesitated at the door. 'I'm all right. All I needed was a bit of a lie-down. My head's not going to be too bad, thank goodness.'

Louise sat on a chair beside the bed. 'It was a wonderful ceremony,' she said.

Amber smiled. 'Yes, wasn't it?' Then she burst out emotionally, 'Louise, you can't imagine how relieved I am now that it's all over! It's been an intolerable strain this past few months. But at last I'm free . . .'

Louise could think of nothing to say, and Amber went on, 'I felt so proud today, and so sad . . . and yet happy too. Peter will never be forgotten now, Louise.' She smiled again. 'When I saw your portrait hanging there . . . the first time I'd seen it in place . . . it was as though he was really there with us. I don't know how you did it, but you made Peter so real . . . and you never even knew him.'

Louise was pleased, but diffident. 'I was afraid at one time that I wouldn't be able to do it.' She did not, however, want to discuss why, so she went on quickly, 'Amber, you said there was something you wanted to say to me . . .'

Amber suddenly looked as anxious as she had on the stairs earlier, and her eyes shifted away from Louise uneasily. 'Yes . . . it's just that I want you to be the first to know, Louise. I don't want the news to come as a shock to you, from anyone else.'

'Shock?' Louise was mystified.

Amber twisted a corner of the counterpane between her fingers. 'Yes, you see now that this business is over, I feel I can begin to live my own life . . . start again.'

'And of course you should,' Louise agreed, but could not understand why Amber should think she would be shocked. They had talked about it before in an oblique way.

Amber reached for her hand and tentatively touched it. 'Louise, I hope with all my heart you'll forgive me. I didn't want it to happen this way, but I couldn't help myself . . . and neither could he. I'm so afraid you'll be hurt, even though Edgar has assured me . . .'

'Edgar?' echoed Louise, not quite understanding yet.

Amber looked upset. 'Yes, Edgar. We saw a lot of each other when I was in London for those few weeks in summer, and we ... well, we fell in love, and we're going to be married.' She looked at Louise miserably. 'I'm so sorry, Louise ... I confess it was happening even before then, when he was here, but neither of us realised ... and in any case he belonged to you ...'

Louise found her voice. 'He never belonged to me, Amber. We were never in love. Oh, he asked me to marry him, it's true, but we both knew it wasn't really serious.'

Amber half sat up. Her eyes were wide. 'Is that really true, Louise?'

Louise smilingly pressed her hand. 'I swear it. I'm very happy for you, Amber, very happy indeed.' But her thoughts were racing. What about Roland? This must be the reason for his dejection. Amber had rejected him for Edgar.

Amber said wistfully, 'I shall hate leaving the Château des Ormeaux, of course, but it will be for the best. The ghost of Peter is always with me here, and besides, Roland must lead his own life, not have it cluttered up with us. One day I hope he'll marry ...' She trailed off, and Louise thought, 'Yes, perhaps, when he gets over losing you for the second time, he might turn to Chantal ...' She could imagine the girl's look of triumph when she heard Amber's news.

They talked for a while about Amber's and Edgar's plans, and then Amber said she felt well enough to get up for dinner. Louise returned to her own room to change. She wore the cherry red dress which she had brought purposely, hoping it would help to cheer her up. As she brushed her dark hair and added a little colour to her pale cheeks, she could only think of Roland and his bitter disappointment.

After all he had done for Amber, his devotion, to

lose her ... And yet alongside her sympathy for Roland, she was also happy for Amber and Edgar. They were perfectly suited, she thought, surprised she had not noticed it before. She smiled to herself. There had been little signs during those days when Edgar had stayed here, and later when she had kept bumping into Amber at the Profile, but she had never paid any attention. Their love had been growing, and she had not noticed. Just as no one had noticed how she was falling in love with Roland, she thought ruefully.

When she went downstairs to the drawing room, only Roland was there, standing morosely by the fireplace in which a fire was crackling merrily. She recalled the past times when she had encountered him thus, but none had ever made her feel as uncomfortable as now. He had a half empty glass in his hand. He looked up and smiled.

'Hello, Louise.'

'Hello, Roland.'

'Have you recovered from all the brouhaha?'

'Yes. Amber is feeling much better too. She said she'd come down for dinner.' Steeling herself, she said as casually as she could, 'She told me about Edgar.'

'My dear ... I'm sorry.' His eyes were full of sympathy.

She could not allow the misconception to continue now. 'You needn't feel sorry for me. I'm delighted.' His look of amazement was hardly unexpected. She went on, 'There was never any serious relationship between Edgar and me.'

'But I thought ... you gave the impression ...'

'You jumped to conclusions,' Louise told him. 'I was never in love with Edgar. He liked to tease me by asking me to marry him.'

'Nevertheless you let me think . . .' He raked his fingers through his hair. 'And you looked so miserable at the dedication, so abject . . . I thought you must already know, and it was because Edgar had jilted you. I was worrying all the time about you.'

Louise was touched that he had been concerned for her. 'I'm sorry,' she said. Then impulsively she went on, 'I can understand how you feel . . . how bitterly disappointed you must be.' She felt she had clumsily made the understatement of the year.

Roland looked at her with fresh amazement. 'Disappointed? I? I'm not disappointed. I'm delighted. Amber isn't a woman who should spend her life alone. Edgar is just right for her.'

It was Louise's turn for amazement. 'But, Roland, I thought you expected to marry her. I mean, everyone said you used to be in love with her, and it was just a matter of time . . .'

A smile curved around his lips. 'How the gossips love to remember! Yes, I confess I was captivated by her when I was younger, as Peter was, but it wasn't love. Do you think I could have stayed here all these years watching another man with the woman I loved?'

'You might,' Louise ventured.

'You don't know me!' he said feelingly. 'No, I'm not in love with Amber, haven't been for years. I'm very fond of her and despite our clashes of will I think she's fond of me. She takes my advice more often than not, although she hates to admit it. She never loved me. Oh, sometimes we used to joke about getting married, in the same way as you and Edgar perhaps, because it would have been a convenient solution to the situation . . .'

'But I heard her say to you that even Peter approved . . .' Louise broke in, and then guiltily remembered how she had been eavesdropping.

Roland's eyebrows rose. 'Was that the night of the party at the General's?'

Louise nodded.

'She'd been very depressed that day,' Roland said, 'and she turned to me for advice. She was in a very emotional state, and I know why now. She was starting to fall in love with Edgar. She already knew him, don't forget, and when he came down here she suddenly became restive, but I don't think she realised why herself until some time later. Peter always used to say jokingly that if anything happened to him, Amber would be all right because she could marry me. I think he meant it, but love doesn't always oblige for convenience. Amber was never in love with me—otherwise she wouldn't have married Peter.' He studied Louise's attentive face searchingly. 'So why, Louise, are you looking so miserable, if Edgar's marrying Amber doesn't upset you?'

Louise felt her colour rising. 'So why are you?' she countered.

'Because I believed the girl I want to marry couldn't possibly want to marry me,' he said slowly.

Chantal, thought Louise. She must be playing hard to get for once—but now she can't lose. Oh, what did he see in a superficial girl like her? Chantal was beautiful, of course . . .

She said resolutely, 'Have you asked her?'

'Not yet.'

'Well then, why don't you? I expect that's all she's waiting for.'

To her astonishment he held out his hands, grasped hers and pulled her firmly into the circle of his arms.

His deep grey eyes looked at her from under their lush dark lashes, and a muscle at the corner of his mouth quivered uncertainly, as he asked softly, 'Will you marry me, Louise?'

For a moment her heart seemed to stop beating. He was joking. He must be. But his eyes were burning into hers and the message in them was startlingly clear. She hardly dared believe it.

'Me?' she whispered.

'You, my darling. The most beautiful, desirable girl in the world. I'll marry no other.'

Louise could only murmur, 'Yes . . . oh, Roland . . . yes!'

His mouth prevented her saying more. His lips searched hers hungrily as he held her close, his fingers straying into her hair as they rocked together on the carpet, swaying with the intensity of their emotions.

'Louise . . . Louise . . .' he breathed, 'I love you!'

'I love you too, Roland!' She answered breathlessly.

His lips merged with hers once more, and they were lost in each other for a long long moment. Only the sound of the door opening made them jerk guiltily apart. Amber and Edgar stood open-mouthed in the doorway. Nobody spoke for a full minute, then Roland shattered the silence, his face breaking into a broad smile.

'Come in, come in . . . don't stand there gawping. Louise and I have something rather important to tell you.'

Amber and Edgar advanced across the room. Amber looked from one to the other incredulously. 'You don't mean . . . yes, you do mean!' She rushed towards them and hugged them both. 'Oh, my dears, it it really true? You're in love?'

Louise blushed happily, and Roland said emphatically, 'And going to be married.'

Edgar said drily, 'I thought there was something the matter with Louise. She's been like a zombie these past months.'

'And I thought she'd be upset because of us,' said Amber. 'And Roland thought so too, didn't you?'

'Well, I thought Roland was going to marry you,' put in Louise.

Amber exploded into laughter. She kissed Louise's cheek. 'What a silly bunch of idiots we've been! I'm so happy it's turned out like this. I couldn't imagine a nicer wife for Roland than you.' She threw him an impish glance. 'Louise will keep you in order, Roland. She won't stand any nonsense.'

Roland looked lovingly down at Louise and his arm around her shoulders tightened. His eyes narrowed a fraction, as he teased, ' I know that—only too well!'

Edgar said, 'I hope this won't be the end of your career as a portrait painter, Louise.'

Louise looked questioningly up at Roland. The teasing look came back into his eyes as he said, 'Definitely not. There'll still be children around for her to paint portraits of, I'm sure!'

Louise blushed furiously as they all laughed.

Then Amber said, 'Well now, this calls for a celebration. Champagne. We must have lots of champagne.' Impulsively she hugged them again, and then Edgar in whose arms she stayed. 'This is going to be a day to remember!'

Louise pressed close to Roland, and he held her tightly against him. It was indeed going to be a day to remember, she thought. The happiest day of her life.

THE FATHER OF IMPRESSIONISM

Impressionism is a style of painting outdoor subjects, and is characterized by bold strokes of bright color. Seen close up an Impressionist picture with its thick patches of paint makes little sense. But from a short distance the scene falls into place and the painting flickers and vibrates, as if in motion.

Claude Monet, hailed today as the father of Impressionism, was born in 1840 and grew up in the French port city of Le Havre. At nineteen, he settled in Paris to paint, and here began an extended period of hardship.

To save on rent, Monet built a studio-boat from which he painted variations of sunlight and mist on water and riverbank. Friends came to paint with him, Renoir among them, and in 1874 a group of these artists arranged an exhibition in Paris. The response to the group's work ranged from sarcasm to outrage. A critic mockingly called the artists "impressionists," after the title of Monet's painting *Impression: Sunrise*. The artists adopted the label.

Despite extreme poverty and the death of his beloved wife, Monet continued to paint his serene landscapes. By 1880, after almost thirty years of struggle and criticism, Monet finally began to break through to the public. He moved to a country house and settled down to paint willows, water lilies and exotic flowers—often extensive series of single subjects captured at different moments of the day.

In 1923 Monet was nearly blind, yet he continued to paint right up to the time of his death in 1926 ... forever capturing on canvas his poetic impressions of the beauty of nature.